# Budc

'Bullies Beware

or

You will face me to give you a scare'

## Ralph Brammer

*Other books by Ralph Brammer*
UK: 'Football Skills'
USA: 'Soccer Skills & Drills'
Poland: 'Pilka Nozna'

Cover design: Campbell Haig Ltd, Dunstable LU5 5AS –
campbellhaig@mac.com
Editing/Proofing: Jane Hammett – www. jane-hammett.co.uk
Desktop Publishing: Pageset Ltd, High Wycombe, Bucks.
Printed and bound in Great Britain by Clays Ltd, St Ives plc.

British Library Cataloguing in Publication Data is available from
the British Library

ISBN: 978-1-9998126-0-7

# Acknowledgements

Editor Jane Hammett. Her professional expertise was invaluable throughout.

Campbell Haig for his proficient ability in graphic design.

Nigel Austin for his expert typesetting.

Special thanks to my wonderful wife Heather for her input and support.

# A word from the author

My first book *Football Skills* was published in 2000, and is still in print today.

I wrote the story *Buddy Wizard* several years ago, primarily as an interest. Recently, I decided to revamp the book into an all gender story, which I hope readers will enjoy.

# Buddy Wizard

# Chapter 1

He crept slowly along the candlelit tunnels beneath the medieval castle, glancing cautiously at the flickering flames and the shadows that drifted along the jagged stone walls. Distant voices were a constant reminder that he wasn't alone in this unearthly maze of dungeons. He was only a boy, without weapons or guidance. Was this a test of his skill, cunning or bravery? What creatures lurked in this damp, narrow tomb? Would this evil place soon become his grave?

He could taste the damp, mouldy air and repeatedly licked his parched lips. He longed for a glass of cool water, the comforts of home, and to return to the twenty-first century.

Warily, he ventured on, into the creepy unknown, and began to climb a set of steep, winding stone steps. Beads of sweat trickled down his back as he climbed higher and higher up the long, dark stairway. Suddenly, a light flickered, sunlight dazzled him, and he stepped into a large hall with arched windows and high ceilings. His eyes focused on dust particles floating aimlessly towards him from a doorway at the far end of the room. A cool breeze stroked his face. He gathered his strength and ran frantically from the dungeons. He pounded forward, eagerly anticipating his escape. Suddenly, a deafening roar echoed all around. A huge figure sprang through the doorway, blocking his only path to freedom. Daniel froze in his tracks, his heart thumping in his chest. A shiver swept through his body as he stood, rigid, glancing at the shadowy figure. Trembling, he looked up, focusing on the ugly man-like creature with its blue, wrinkled face, long, straggly hair, and bloodshot eyes. The creature glared down at him and snarled.

Then, without warning, a loud noise broke the silence.

'Daniel! Daniel! Hurry up! You'll be late for school.'

Daniel threw the book down, jumped off the bed and knocked poor Chip flying.

'Sorry, Chip, Sorry, Mum. This wizard book is awesome. I'm coming.'

Mum's voice rang through the air again. 'Come on, you can read later! I don't know – spells, ghosts, magic. That's all you ever think of!'

Daniel hopped around the bedroom with one leg in his trousers. 'Sorry, Mum, I just got carried away.' He fumbled into his shirt, laughing. He carefully picked up his little dog and cuddled him. 'It's okay, Chip, but I wonder if…' Daniel rushed over to the bedroom window and looked down into the garden. They watched as a small robin hopped along the soft layer of white, then Daniel pointed.

'Look, more snow, Chip. The food is covered up – we'd better put some more out, or the birds will die.'

Daniel was a quiet twelve-year-old who liked

reading. He wasn't exactly the intellectual type – far from it! He preferred science-fiction and fantasy. He was an imaginative boy, regarded as a daydreamer by everyone, including his mum and dad. But who were they to comment? Even Mr and Mrs Brady's neighbours considered them to be eccentric workaholics. Daniel's teenage sister, Emily, was a self-centred troll, thought Daniel, and best ignored. The smallest member of the household, but the most important (as far as Daniel was concerned), was Chip, his faithful little dog and the only one in the house he could relate to.

Daniel moved quickly that morning and jogged down the stairs, his hair bobbing up and down as he went. Little Chip followed close behind. He dived straight into the kitchen, sneaked some biscuits, then stepped quietly out to the cold garden.

'Stay, Chip! Stay, there's a good boy. Don't frighten the robin.' Gently, Daniel cleared the snow from the top of the garden wall, while the little dog's eyes keenly followed the pieces of biscuit that Daniel scattered on the wall. Suddenly, the kitchen door swung open and Mum's voice beckoned him again.

'Daniel! Come on, hurry up, and don't you dare bring that snow in here.'

Instantly, the robin flew off, skimming low to the ground before fluttering swiftly out of sight.

'Mum, you scared it.'

But the kitchen door had already closed. Daniel looked down sadly. He handed Chip a biscuit then sighed. 'Never mind, he'll come back. I suppose I'd better go now. I only wish you could come with me.'

It was February, and Daniel was in his second term at Middleton High. He was a newt (which is what Year 7s were called by the older students). His mum usually drove him the ten-minute journey to school. She drove a posh red car, wore matching red lipstick, and didn't give a hoot about other drivers. Today was no exception. In a queue of traffic, Mrs Brady sat cursing. 'Look at that idiot.' She blasted her horn.

Uncomfortable, Daniel sat still, then decided to speak. 'They call that road rage, Mum.'

'It's not me, it's them! They make me in a bad mood.'

As they neared the school, Mrs Brady was driving carelessly.

'Watch out, Mum!' gasped Daniel, but it was too late. She drove through a heap of slush, spraying a group of children. Daniel ducked out of sight until the car came to a halt. Cautiously, he peered through the window then discreetly stepped out onto the pavement.

Within seconds Daniel had blended in with all the other kids heading in the same direction, but he trudged along, thinking, *I hope my mum didn't spray slush over Bullfrog Riley. If she did, I'm dead! I know he'll get me, I know he will. He will. I hate him. I really do.*

*'Brady!'*

Daniel heard his name and instinctively looked up, only to see a white flash, then the cold, painful sting of a snowball hitting his face. He cringed, clutching his face.

'That was a good shot, eh, Brady?' sniggered the same voice.

Daniel opened his blurry eyes to see that his worst nightmare, Bullfrog Riley and the Slippery Geeks, had surrounded him. His stomach churned as he wiped away the snow.

'We don't like posh posers like you,' jeered Riley, turning and grinning at his tall freaky friends, the identical twins. 'What shall we do with him, lads?'

Daniel kept quiet, edging back, but Riley came closer, stalking Daniel. Then another snowball slammed into Daniel's face. The impact knocked him off his feet and he slipped, landing with a thump in the snow.

Footsteps crunched past as Daniel stood up, holding his nose. He brushed the snow from his clothes as other kids strolled past, laughing, until…

'Are you all right?' asked his friend Sophie Little, also known as little Sophie because of her frail appearance, freckly face, and button nose, which didn't help to make her a tough ally. She was a quiet, friendly, intelligent girl with a dry sense of humour, but she was easily intimidated and struggled to challenge more assertive kids.

'I think my nose is broken.' Daniel sniffed gently. 'Is it bleeding?'

Sophie carefully examined his nose. 'No, it's okay.'

'It really hurts.'

Sophie bit her fingernail. 'You should report Riley.'

Daniel wiped away a tear. 'I daren't.'

He flicked the last bits of snow from his coat then sighed. 'I wish I could send him to the depths of a real grotty, putrid place – then ram a snowball down his throat. Anyway, if you saw what happened, why didn't you help me?'

'Sorry, Daniel, but … I'm only a girl and … he *really* freaks me out.'

'Me too. He's always picking on me in class.'

Sophie looked around warily. 'They've gone now. Shall we go?'

Together they walked towards the old school gates of Middleton High. The school was built in the grounds of the former Middleton Manor and castle. The ancient castle had stood alone for centuries, then in late Tudor times Middleton Manor had been built next to it, along with an orphanage, stables and servants' quarters. When the castle and manor fell into decay they were demolished, and the school was constructed, using many of the old bricks and stone from the manor. Its main entrance appeared vaguely similar to the old manor, with an arched stone doorway, high ceilings and wooden beams. Middleton Manor had – apparently – been haunted, and there were rumours that the school was haunted too, but these stories were hushed up to protect the school's image.

Daniel reckoned, based on the ghost stories he'd read, that both good and bad ghosts lingered on at the school and fought each other.

'You don't see the ghosts,' claimed Daniel, 'unless they want you to. But if you do, you become spellbound and are dragged all the way to the castle dungeons – and tortured.'

Sophie cringed. 'I don't believe you. Who told you that?'

Daniel raised his eyebrows. 'It's true.'

'You mean, like good versus evil?'

'Sort of. I read about a school orphanage and men in the eighteenth century who tortured people, including children. They were really bad people. Our school was built where the castle, manor and orphanage stood all those years ago. Apparently there was a prophecy. It says that children who died in the orphanage placed a curse on the wicked people, and one day a descendant of one of the children will lead them to invoke their revenge. And they will seek out and destroy all that is evil, along with anyone who stands in their way. According to this book, the prophecy could be linked to the school. Maybe it could happen at Middleton High. Then they could get Riley.'

Sophie chewed her fingers. 'Sounds like your books could lead you into trouble. That information is a bit scary.'

'It's supposed to scare you – but Riley's scarier – and evil. You're lucky that you hardly see him.'

Sophie looked nervously around. 'Forget him. Shouldn't we go now?'

In the classroom Daniel could feel Riley's presence behind him. Seconds later something hit his ear and a pencil bounced from his desk onto the floor.

Miss White, the English teacher, noticed. 'Pick up your pencil, please, Daniel.'

Daniel stooped to pick it up. 'Okay, Miss, but it's not mine – it's Riley's.' He then muttered under his breath, 'Go to hell, pig.'

Miss White, an elderly teacher who usually smiled a lot, seemed different today. She appeared to be in a bad mood – but her hearing was sharp.

'What did you say, Daniel?'

Daniel gulped, 'Nothing, Miss.'

'I hope you're not being troublesome?' The irritated tone of her voice demanded an answer.

'No, Miss, honest.'

Later that day, as he did every day, Daniel was heading along the school corridor to meet Sophie when an object flew past his ear. A ball of paper dropped to the floor in front of him. He carried on walking, trying to ignore it, but couldn't stop thinking. *Someone threw that at me. It must be Riley? I'll walk faster. Maybe I should run.* Suddenly, he felt a push. He stumbled, lost his balance. His books slipped from his hand and he fell, sprawling onto the floor.

The Geeks stared at Daniel, their thin lips curled in a menacing grin as they laughed and slyly walked past him, kicking his books along the floor. Daniel scrambled after his books.

'Pack it in! Get lost, you two.' He began sobbing as other boys joined in and scuffed his books along the corridor.

'Why are you scrabbling about on the floor, Daniel Brady?' said a voice. Daniel peered up to see the unwelcome plump face of Miss Tubble, the maths teacher.

'I'm only picking up my books, Miss – they were knocked out of my hand.'

'He dropped them, Miss,' interrupted Bullfrog Riley, who was standing nearby. 'He's always dropping them.'

Daniel jumped to his feet, replying angrily, 'Liar.'

Miss Tubble leaned back, placing her hands on her hips. 'Stop daydreaming, Brady, and get to your lesson.'

Daniel gulped as he looked nervously into her piercing green eyes. He then spotted Riley behind her, laughing.

Sheepishly, Daniel fidgeted, noticing the other boys and girls staring at him, before running away along the corridor. The dumbfounded Miss Tubble stared daggers after him. He ran all the way to Sophie, still sobbing. 'Old bat – I hate her and Riley.'

'Bats are friends with Dracula. I bet that's scary too.'

'Yes, just like Tubble. She gives me the creeps sometimes, especially when she gets angry. I reckon the school is creepy and ghostly too.'

'Wizards, witches and now ghosts? I'm glad it's daylight.'

'Today, yeah, but I reckon a corridor like this may have led to some old dungeon. This school is eerie in winter when the lights go out. That's when all the ghosts come alive. I hope they come and get Riley and Tubble.'

To Sophie's relief, the corridor began to fill with pupils heading for their lessons. 'Don't you think we'd better get going?'

Daniel didn't take much notice. 'You go – I'll catch you later.'

She went away, concerned. Glancing back, she saw Daniel staring at a wooden plaque fixed to the wall, one of four that had been rescued from the demolished buildings. Daniel loved the old carved inscriptions and could relate to them. He believed this particular plaque came from the school orphanage, and couldn't resist reciting the words:

*Fear not the task*
*Nor the pain you feel*
*Look to your dreams*
*Your spirit will heal*

# Chapter 2

After school Daniel's mum picked him up and they drove home. Soon, they turned into Old Furrow Way, a quiet, tree-lined road. They passed detached houses with long driveways covered in snow. Lawns, bushes and trees were subtly hidden in white. Daniel glanced at the squirrel sign that greeted them as the car bumped over the kerb and onto the driveway, then came to a sudden halt, centimetres from the garage door. Phew, that was close again, thought Daniel, opening the car door and jumping out.

Once through the front door, a large hallway revealed a prominent staircase. There were doors to the left and right to the lounge and dining room. Ahead was a door leading into the kitchen.

'Mum,' Daniel said quietly, following her, Chip jumping up at his side, 'a boy at school keeps picking on me.'

Mrs Brady's face wore a vacant expression. She tapped across the floor in her high heels and leaned over a big bunch of flowers, poking her nose in the colourful petals. She took a long, sensuous sniff then smiled.

'What did you say, Daniel?' Mrs Brady continued speaking to her flowers as if they could hear her. 'Ah, I must give you some more Troggle feed,' she said, looking at her plants. 'There's a little drop of water for you, and some for you.' She then whispered, 'Let's have a look at the sweeties in the conservatory, shall we?'

Daniel pursued her, Chip close behind. The little dog also wanted some attention, and began to dance on his hind legs, wagging his stubby tail.

'Mum, Mum, a boy nicknamed Bullfrog Riley hit me. Mum! Do you have to talk to those stupid flowers?'

'Sorry,' she replied.

The kitchen and the conservatory contained so many varieties of flowers that every space was filled. Each room resembled an overgrown greenhouse.

Mrs Brady always dressed colourfully. Each day, she wore perfume with a flowery scent to match her flowery dress.

Eventually, Daniel sighed. 'I know you're busy, Mum. But don't forget you promised to take me sledging. I've arranged to meet Sophie there.'

Mum heard that. 'Okay. I know – you want a lift. Take me here – take me there.'

'That was always Emily, not me, Mum. I hardly ever ask.'

Later, in the park, the popular sledge run was buzzing with people, lit up by rows of glowing street lights that shone on the slope. All sizes of toboggans slithered gracefully down, carrying excited children, including Daniel and Sophie. But Daniel had something else on his mind and each time they walked back up the slope he would comment, 'I hate Riley.'

Sophie sighed. 'Try to keep out of his way.'

'How can I? He's in my class.'

'Report him, then.'

Daniel wiped a tear from his eye. 'He'll just pick on me even more.'

Little Chip scampered through the snow and ran in circles around Daniel. Mrs Brady, however, continued to stand, shivering, next to Sophie's dad.

'How long have we got to stand here for?' she called out.

'Not long, Mum. Just let me give Chip a ride.' Daniel pulled Chip along on the sledge in between the other children. Everyone laughed. He ran with the sledge to the sound of cheers, but then spotted a familiar silhouette in the distance and stopped. 'Oh no, Chip! I just thought I saw Riley.'

The little dog stood up, growling, as three shadows approached. Luckily, they turned and went the other way. Daniel remained uneasy. 'Riley was here, Sophie. I think he's trying to scare me. He called me a posh poser, but I'm not – I'm just a bit smarter than him. He gets things wrong in school and he was fuming the other day. I laughed a bit – I shouldn't have, but so did others. He went bright red then glared at me.'

'You probably embarrassed him. A similar thing happened to me. A girl put her nose right up to my face then poked her tongue out at me. She laughed with her friend. I hate her!'

The next morning saw little change in the weather. Again Daniel's mum took him to school. But a carefully planned delaying tactic enabled him to arrive ten minutes later than usual. He hoped to avoid Bullfrog Riley in the playground.

Daniel stepped out of his mum's car and ran along the snow-covered pavement towards the school gates. Only a handful of boys and girls remained near the entrance as Daniel stopped before heading cautiously through. No Riley, he thought, increasing his pace. Suddenly, someone grabbed him. His heart missed a beat. He swung around.

'Sorry, it's only me,' Sophie said frantically. 'I had to stop you – Bullfrog Riley is over there.'

Daniel stood still, straining his eyes left and right. 'Where?' he asked hastily.

'He hasn't seen us yet.'

Daniel shuffled nervously towards Sophie. 'You'd better not be kidding me.'

'I'm not kidding – I'm scared. You said I wouldn't get picked on in this school.'

'It's not you, it's me they're after because of Riley.' Suddenly Daniel felt something hit his back. *Not again!*

'Nerd!' a girl shouted.

'Snob!' a boy yelled.

Then without warning came a flurry of snowballs. Daniel and Sophie felt the snowballs pummel their heads and backs as they ran for safety.

Daniel's first lesson of the day was maths with Miss Tubble. He sat quietly at his desk, opened his book and shuddered in disbelief at the first page, which was covered in black smudges. He glanced first at Riley, then at Miss Tubble. He had to report Riley for this – but would Miss Tubble believe him? *She seems okay, but I don't think she likes me. She might throw a wobbly, or shout, or – worse still – laugh, or...* Hesitantly, he raised his hand.

'Excuse me, Miss.'

Break-time soon arrived. A relieved Daniel was eager to find Sophie and tell her he had reported Riley. He darted quickly around the building, dodged in and out of the other kids, and slid in the snow, until he came to a sudden halt.

'Sorry,' Daniel mumbled nervously, realising to his horror he had bumped into Bullfrog Riley. 'I didn't see you.'

Riley glared at Daniel with his cold grey eyes. 'Tough!' he said. 'You little creep.'

Daniel didn't answer. He trembled at Riley's big nostrils snorting steam into the cold air. The red-faced Riley sneered. 'Who told Miss Tubble I smudged your book?'

Daniel froze, his mouth wide open, then took a step backwards. 'Leave me alone ... or else.'

Riley laughed, framed by his friends, the Slippery Geeks. 'Or else what, Brady?' He sneakily stepped on Daniel's foot and kicked him.

Daniel held his arms rigid by his side, his face pale as pain shot through his toes. His eyes glistened. He clutched at his shin with both hands before shouting,

'You fat coward!'

Riley's eyes narrowed. 'What did you call me?'

A small crowd of boys and girls had gathered, not wanting to draw attention to themselves, but trying to get a better view of the action.

'Hey, break it up! Break it up, you lot,' bellowed Miss Tubble, barging through a group of children and brushing them aside like skittles. She glowered at all the pupils. 'What's going on here?'

'I'll tell you, Miss,' said Tyler Topping, a tall, intelligent-looking black boy in glasses.

Riley held up his leg. 'He kicked me, Miss, so I kicked him back.'

'That's a lie,' Daniel mumbled, pulling his trouser leg up to reveal what he thought was going to be a whopping great bruise, but there was only a small scratch.

The dumpy Miss Tubble spun round, flapping her arms impatiently like a goose, shooing the children away. 'Break-time is over – now get back to your classes.' She waited for everyone to disperse before waddling briskly away, leaving Daniel to struggle to his feet, his shin throbbing.

The boys' cloakroom was a safe haven for Daniel. He bathed his leg with only minutes to spare before he was due back in class. He crouched, cursing under his breath. 'My leg really hurts.'

'Catch!' a boy shouted. But before Daniel could turn around, something wet and heavy landed on his head. He snatched the object then inspected it. 'Oh, no, it's my coat.' Daniel hobbled past rows of coats until he reached number 112 and saw his vacant peg. He slumped onto the bench and sat staring at his sodden coat.

'Who's in here?' called another voice. 'Oh, it's you, Daniel,' said the surprised Mr Shaw, the short, balding PE teacher. 'Shouldn't you be in class?'

'Yes, sir, but I've just found my coat all covered in slush.' Daniel dangled the wet coat in his outstretched hand. 'Look, sir.'

Mr Shaw peered at it over the top of his glasses. 'Yes, I can see that. How did it happen?' But before Daniel could speak, Mr Shaw spoke again. 'Look, Daniel, we'll discuss this later. You should be in class by now, so run along, there's a good lad.'

Daniel hung the coat on his peg then wandered despondently out of the cloakroom, his head bowed. He didn't get very far along the corridor before he reached the plaque. He stopped, focusing on the words:

*Fear not the task*
*Nor the pain you feel*
*Look to your dreams*
*Your spirit will heal.*

Daniel mooched along, taking comfort from the plaque, deep in thought. *The words on the plaque are the same as how I feel. It must have been a lot worse in that orphanage.*

It took him a while to reach the classroom. On entering the room, Daniel was confronted by an angry Miss White.

'Where have you been, Daniel?' she asked sternly.

'You're ten minutes late.'

'Sorry, Miss, but I went to the cloakroom and—'

Miss White was impatient. 'Sit down, please, Daniel; we can't have you wandering all over the school.'

The other students laughed as Daniel bowed his head before sitting down awkwardly.

Riley muttered, 'Nerd.'

Miss White intervened. 'Stop that.'

Daniel always sat with a mixture of boys and girls, but none were his real friends – not like Sophie. He often compared the children to cartoon characters, matching a few to funny shapes and faces. He liked drawing and sketched caricatures of his classmates – with the exception of Riley. He drew him as a monster, and kept those drawings hidden. Sophie was often in another group and Daniel didn't see that much of her, but he kept hoping that next term or in Year 8 they could sit together in the same class.

\*\*\*

That evening, Daniel sat unhappily at the dining table, listening to a boring conversation between his parents. He looked at his mum, who wore a brightly coloured jumper. She always craved attention. He then glanced at his dad, who wore an old-fashioned striped shirt and had a droopy moustache. Mr Brady was a perfectionist, a self-absorbed character who took pride in his work, but Daniel imagined him as a lord of the manor.

'You design cars, don't you, Dad?'

'Yes, I do, son.'

'Then why are you building a crappy old car in the garage?'

'Don't ask silly questions,' tutted Mum. 'It's a vintage model.'

Daniel picked up his book, which was titled *Alien Family,* then said, 'But he's always out there.' He switched his attention back to his dad. 'If I built a car, I'd build one that's fast or one that flies into the future, like, you know, what's his name…'

Mum butted in. 'Honestly, Daniel, those books of yours.'

'Leave it out, Mum.'

Daniel studied his mum and dad and wondered which one he most resembled. He was sure his dad dyed his hair because it was such an unusual colour. Daniel had noticed that his mum and dad argued a lot. He thought it might be because of him. He knew they had some good points, but couldn't remember what they were. He listened to his mum gossip about the neighbours then listened to his dad talk about a brand-new car, until he couldn't wait any longer.

'Dad, I'm not happy at school. A boy kicked me today.'

'Stand up for yourself, son. I remember when I was a boy…'

That was it: time for Daniel to switch off. He thought of his favourite television programme, *Teenage Trouble,* but just then trouble arrived in the shape of Emily.

'Kick him back.' His sixteen-year-old sister Emily

laughed as she sat at the table.

'Don't get into trouble,' Mum replied.

'Kick him back,' Emily scoffed again, flicking her hair over her shoulder. 'I would.'

Poor little Chip didn't like all the talking. He covered his ears with his paws.

Daniel listened to all three trying to convince him each had the right answer, until he became sick of listening to them. He got up without saying a word then ran out of the room, closely followed by Chip. Everything went quiet, except for Emily's voice.

'What's up with him lately?'

'I'd like to turn Riley and the Geeks into goblins like these,' Daniel sighed, sitting on his bed, pointing to the pictures in his book. 'Emily is only interested in her appearance, and Mum and Dad say it's just part of growing up. But you'll help me, Chip, won't you?'

Little Chip whined and tilted his head from side to side.

\*\*\*

Riley was now the informal leader of a group of girls and boys who regularly taunted Daniel and Sophie. They had formed a sort of gang that you were either with or against. Most pupils in Year 7 were subtly enticed to become friends with Riley – or felt they had little choice in the matter. Daniel, however, was not part of this group, nor was he considered a friend. He, therefore, remained an enemy and a target.

# Chapter 3

Daniel sat in his mum's car, waiting to go to school. It was spring, and the front garden of their house was alive with flowers budding. The lawn extended out to meet a row of small bushes that indicated the edge of the property. Shrubs were laced with spider webs, and droplets of dew dangled precariously from each strand.

'Clunk click, with every trip,' sang Mrs Brady as she slammed the car door, started the engine and shot off the driveway before turning on to the road. The car sped along as Daniel gazed vacantly out of the window at the pink petals of a magnolia tree, people hurrying along the pavements, and the sunlight flashing through the tall, leafy trees until he arrived at school.

Daniel sat through his first lesson without incident, but then it was PE. He buried his head in his kit bag. 'Where are my trainers? They're missing.'

'Perhaps you forgot them,' Tim Dalton commented, a boy with freckles and protruding ears.

Frantically, Daniel emptied his kit bag. 'I always leave them at school – they've disappeared.'

'I saw some trainers in the trees near the playing fields,' said another boy.

'I bet they're mine.' Daniel frowned. He looked for

Mr Shaw and asked frantically, 'Please, sir, can I go and get my trainers?'

'Yes, okay, Daniel – but be quick about it.'

Daniel hurried off to the trees that ran along the edge of the school playing fields – an area that was out of bounds to all pupils, but easily visible from the classrooms. He searched until he spotted his trainers tied together and caught in the branches of a tree. Luckily, the tree had lots of low branches, and seemed easy to climb. Daniel didn't waste any time scrambling up. Then, step by step, he climbed higher and higher towards his trainers.

'Got them,' he said at last, puffing. He began to edge his way back to the trunk then stopped. He could see something strange. Smoke drifted from the tree trunk. He heard a sizzle. He panicked. Was the tree on fire? His eyes focused on more puffs of smoke, then small red glowing letters began to appear in the wood. The words *Touch me to see* appeared. Daniel crouched, spellbound, watching as more letters appeared, one after the other. They burned a clear message into the wood, which read:

*Touch me to see*
*My words unlock me.*

Daniel scrambled away, suddenly afraid. 'I'm not touching that – I'm out of here.' Frantically, he clambered away.

Suddenly, Mr Shaw's voice echoed through the branches. 'Get down this instant, Brady.'

Daniel jumped out of his skin and let go of his

trainers. They hit the branches before tumbling to the ground. His legs quivered. 'Y-y-yes, sir, I-I-I'm coming.' He edged awkwardly down the branches as Mr Shaw looked up.

A large crowd of boys in their PE kits, including Riley, had gathered and were shuffling closer, with Mr Shaw signalling them to stand back.

Mr Shaw called up. 'Okay, Daniel, you're doing fine.'

Daniel descended carefully.

'Phew, this is hard work,' Mr Shaw muttered.

Riley waited alongside the Geeks, laughing. 'Jump, Brady,' he hollered. 'I'll catch you.'

At that moment Daniel's left foot slipped. Everyone gasped as he let go of the branch and swung in mid-air. He dangled perilously, holding on with his right hand.

'Hold tight,' Mr Shaw shouted, wiping the sweat from his forehead. 'Now lift your left foot up and place it back on the branch.'

Without hesitation Daniel lifted his foot back on the branch then followed Mr Shaw's instructions the rest of the way to the ground.

For the remainder of that day Daniel felt uneasy. *Had he really had seen words appear in the tree trunk?*

Sophie held Daniel's hand when he told her about it. 'Are you sure you didn't imagine it? I'd have been really spooked.'

'I *was* spooked. It was really freaky up there.'

# Chapter 4

The next few weeks passed. Nothing changed. Riley continued to persecute Daniel and Sophie – and he turned up when they least expected him. They tried to keep out of his way, but the persistent Riley enjoyed seeing them suffer and making their life at school miserable.

At home, Daniel read up on wizards and ghosts, trying to piece together more clues about Middleton Manor, the words etched in the tree, and his theories. Chip, who was a great listener, always cocked his ears whenever Daniel spoke, or read out loud, as though he understood each word. He was a smart little dog who could detect Daniel's moods, which over the past few months had sunk to an all-time low.

Daniel looked into Chip's brown eyes. 'I wish I could make Riley disappear, Chip, and the sooner the better.'

Chip gave a small whine as if to agree. Daniel stared at the floor. 'I don't want to go to school, Chip. I want to run away.'

\*\*\*

The sun lazed over Middleton High and small white

clouds floated in a clear blue sky. The temperature hit the twenties, hinting that the weeks ahead could lead into a hot summer. Daniel stood in the playground with Sophie, staring at the east side of the school building. It rose to ten times their height, its castle-like walls towering up to a steep black slate roof. Daniel glanced over the rooftop and gazed at the clouds. He became fascinated by the patterns that emerged, unaware of the boys and girls who had gathered to taunt him.

Riley turned up and stood jeering. 'Look, there's doom and gloom.'

'Sad Sophie,' said a girl.

Daniel and Sophie didn't hang around. They slunk away inside the school, to the safe haven of the east corridor, where Daniel stopped to look, once again, at another plaque.

'I believe this plaque is probably from the school orphanage too. I'm going to write these inscriptions down, Sophie. I'm sure they mean something.'

She just had to warn him. 'You'd better watch out. Riley keeps spreading rumours about you. If anyone else knows what you're doing, they'll lock us both up.'

'That's it! A key – to perhaps unlock something. But what? Or is it just a school motto?' With no hesitation, Daniel recited the words on the plaque:

*Study to learn*
*And listen to hear*
*The greatest of tasks*
*You must conquer, not fear.*

'I like the idea of conquering fear, don't you Sophie?'

'Yes, of course, but we should go now.'

Suddenly, they heard a voice. 'Why are you in here?'

Daniel and Sophie jumped as Miss Griffin, the tall history teacher, approached and stooped over them. She had dark eyes, drawn cheeks and a hooked nose. 'And why, may I ask, are you reciting the words on that plaque?'

Sophie stepped smartly back behind Daniel. 'I'm not, Miss – I've just come in from the playground.'

Miss Griffin promptly switched her attention. 'And you, Brady?'

'Witches, Miss – I mean, I mean...' Daniel went cold, waiting for the ground to swallow him up. He stood rooted to the spot. 'Sorry, Miss – I meant I'm learning about witches in history.'

Miss Griffin gazed at the walls of the corridor, looking, seemingly deep in thought, at the plaque and the noticeboards. Sophie tried to sneak away, but stopped when Griffin spoke. 'I've heard you're causing trouble, Brady, and telling fibs. Is that true?'

Daniel bowed his head, 'No, Miss, it's not true.'

Griffin scowled. 'You shouldn't be in here. Outside, now!'

Sophie scurried away, stumbling through the doorway, but to Miss Griffin's obvious annoyance, Daniel took his time.

Sophie turned to Daniel. 'Everyone's after us now.'

'I know. It's my fault, Sophie, but Griffin's just a witch.'

'I should have seen her coming, Daniel.'

Daniel kicked a stone. 'It's not your fault. Anyway, it'll soon be the end of term.'

'Does that mean we won't see Bullfrog Riley for a while?'

'What did you call me?' Riley said, having crept up alongside them.

Daniel and Sophie looked at each other, glanced at Riley, then ran. They dodged into the school then sprinted along the east corridor, through the crossover link, and kept running into the north corridor, until Sophie came to a sudden halt.

'Wait a minute, I've got a stitch.'

'It's okay,' puffed Daniel, looking back. 'He hasn't followed.'

They caught their breath and continued cautiously along the corridor towards the exit until Daniel spotted something.

'Wait – let's look again at this orphanage plaque.'

Sophie frowned. 'What now?'

Daniel didn't answer. Instead he read the words:

*Fear not the task*
*Nor the pain you feel*
*Look to your dreams*
*Your spirit will heal.*

He grabbed a crumpled piece of paper from his pocket and showed it to Sophie. 'That's it, look! *Touch me to see. My words unlock me.* I wrote these words down after seeing them being burned into the tree.'

Sophie's eyes switched from Daniel to the plaque. 'We're going to get into trouble hanging around here.'

'Sophie, don't you realise? 'My words' must mean the orphan's words – and the orphan wants to be unlocked. So the orphan is trapped somewhere. The plaque came from the orphanage. The orphans are all dead. Could it be one of their spirits that sent a message to me, through the tree?'

'What? I hope not. It's your imagination.'

Daniel rubbed his fingers over the writing on the plaque, reciting the words over and over: *Touch me to see. My words unlock me.* But nothing happened. 'I don't get it,' he said.

In the meantime, Riley was sneaking along the corridor, almost upon them.

Daniel kept rubbing the plaque. He turned to face Sophie, then the plaque magically began to shine. A whisper of smoke drifted out of the plaque and into his jacket pocket. Sophie screamed. Then Daniel spotted Riley. Only one thing was on their mind – running. They sprinted so fast along the corridor that they ran straight into Miss Tubble.

'Why are you two running?' she asked. 'Stop!'

Sophie was quick to answer: 'Riley was after us, Miss.'

'Well, where is he now?' she snapped. They looked for Riley, but he had gone. Miss Tubble laughed. 'Go and wait outside the headmaster's office now, both of you!'

Mr North, the headmaster, was a tall, austere, stocky man with grey hair – a bossy person disliked even by the teachers. It was no surprise to Daniel that he dismissed their story as a load of nonsense and gave them both a lecture on behaviour and a letter to take home to their parents. Daniel shoved his letter where he considered it belonged – in the bin. Sophie, on the other hand, was too scared to discard the letter.

# Chapter 5

Later that evening Daniel lay quietly in his bedroom. The walls were plastered with posters of spy films and footballers. He clasped his hands behind his neck and raised his head from his pillow, looking first at his television screen then at the books that lay scattered across his desk. Casting his eyes further to the left, he saw his rucksack leaning against the wardrobe. It had a full-length mirror, reflecting his bedroom door. He glanced into the mirror and the door opened.

'Had a good day at school, Daniel?' asked his dad.

Daniel thought of the headmaster's letter that he had thrown away, and gulped.

'I'm scared of someone, Dad. He tore a page from my science book today.'

'Don't mess about – get your own back; tear a page from his book.'

Mum peered around the edge of the door. 'Goodnight, dear.'

My mum and dad are weird, thought Daniel. They ask me how I'm getting on at school, but never listen when I tell them. He saw his reflection in the television screen. 'That's it, Chip. I'm going to get Riley somehow. The school plaques mention a spirit – I know the spirit of someone means their strength and character, but it could also mean a ghost spirit. Perhaps it's the ghost of the north or south, east or west. I hope Riley is tortured.' Daniel rolled off his bed, sat at his desk and looked cautiously at the bedroom door then at his watch. Chip sat next to him on the stool, his paw resting on the desk.

'I know it's late, Chip, but where's that book, *Ancient Spells?*' Daniel crawled under the bed, his feet waving. Chip watched him intently.

'Got it,' he said, wriggling back and standing up. 'Don't forget, Chip, this is our secret.' He flicked through the pages while Chip studied them too. 'Let's try to find the part in the book about the prophecy. Sophie said she felt something and noticed that the plaque shone when I rubbed it. Riley crept up on us, so I stopped rubbing it and turned to Riley. I had my back to it when the plaque shone – that's why I didn't see it!'

There were lots of spells in the book and Daniel read for an hour, reciting some and laughing at others, until he came across the prophecy. 'There's even a bit about Middleton Castle again. Look, Chip – it says magicians and witches have existed for many centuries. It mentions castles and magicians going back to medieval times. Then it describes the men at Middleton Manor in the eighteenth century who tortured people, including children. They were real bullies, Chip. It says that the children cursed their torturers, and vowed they'd seek revenge. Maybe something will happen at Middleton High, Chip. At least I'd get my own back on Riley.'

It was past midnight when the whisper of smoke from the school plaque silently crept from Daniel's jacket pocket. It floated along the floor, towards the bed, past Chip, then an eerie mist emerged. The image of a teenage boy appeared, shining in the darkness. He was barefoot, dressed in rags, and looking towards Daniel. He slowly raised one hand. A light shone out into the room. The frightened Chip scampered under the bed. The boy ghost walked closer to Daniel, who was in a deep sleep.

'You reached out for me. I am a spirit of the orphanage.'

Daniel cautiously lowered the covers. 'D-d-did I?'

The strange, shining, straggly-haired boy spoke again. 'We have been waiting for you.'

'You have?'

Daniel's voice trembled. 'Who sent you? Billy Riley?'

The glowing boy laughed. 'No. Don't be afraid.'

'I *am* afraid. What's going to happen to me?'

'You must follow me.' The boy beckoned Daniel with his glittering finger. 'Come,' he said softly.

Daniel stepped from his bed and followed the boy. A small light shone from the boy's finger towards Daniel. The light grew brighter, then in a blinding flash they both disappeared.

'Where are we?' Daniel asked. He was in what seemed like a medieval hall with its high arched beams, bare wooden floors, colourful armour and chalices.

'You are in the hall of justice,' came a voice from behind him.

Daniel spun around and saw the ragged boy again. He was pale, no older than sixteen, and covered in dust. Daniel looked away, then back again. *Am I dreaming?* The boy's eyes sparkled and his face began to change colour. A bright light filled the air. 'Are you a ghost?' Daniel asked.

'Yes, a ghost for all eternity, but I'm also your buddy.'

Suddenly, Daniel found himself standing before a wall of stone. He noticed a carving of two clasped hands, holding a cross. The walls shook and the ghost spoke again. 'This is where your journey begins, and so shall it end.' A fierce wind erupted. Daniel flew into a blinding light. He held out his hands for protection, but somehow disappeared through the wall. He stood in a glittering ray of light … and out of the brightness sprang something horrible. Daniel jumped with fright, looking around anxiously for help, but no one was there except Bullfrog Riley, laughing and kicking dust into the air.

'Clear off, Riley, or I'll…'

'Or you'll what?' Riley replied, grinning nastily.

Suddenly, loud thuds reverberated through the ground and footsteps appeared in the dust. A huge ghost-like creature materialised next to Riley, towering above him. The massive beast of a man stooped, howling.

'Or else, Billy Riley…' echoed his deep voice, 'Or else you will face me!'

Riley remained motionless, staring up at the giant ghost.

33

Daniel edged away backwards and tripped. Then he was thrust up in the air and floated hopelessly around. He heard loud, sinister laughing followed by the deep words: 'Tell all to beware! They will face me, and I will give them a scare.'

'Help,' Daniel gasped, looking down at the ground. He could see his school. 'Help!' he yelled, as he began to fall. 'Help!'

His school loomed closer and closer. In a split second he found himself in a room. He stared in amazement at an open fireplace with a roaring fire that crackled and hissed. Two chairs sat on either side of an old grandfather clock. He wiped the sleep from his eyes, pulled his pyjamas up, then touched the small couch he was standing behind. Near him was the shining boy ghost, who was barefoot and wore torn, tattered clothes as before. Daniel looked up and gazed through a leaded window out onto a street.

'Who's that?' he asked, looking at a man in a bowler hat walking past the window. 'He looks like Mr Penny, the crazy scientist. I've seen him in my books.'

The ghost didn't answer. Instead, a door creaked open. Mr Shaw, the PE teacher entered, wearing a fancy blue waistcoat, followed by Miss White, Daniel's English teacher. Daniel tried to get their attention. 'Mr Shaw, Miss White? It's me!' But, try as he may, they ignored Daniel and sat in the chairs on either side of the clock.

The ghost held up his hand. 'Shush. They can't hear you.'

Mr Shaw scratched his balding head. 'Something is

34

going on at school. It involves Daniel.'

Daniel turned to the ghost. 'They're talking about me.'

Miss White spoke in a soft voice. 'I have heard there are a number of troublemakers in the school. I hope this hasn't anything to do with Daniel?'

Daniel leaned forward and tried to interrupt. 'I told you lot, but nothing happened.' He waited for an answer, but none came.

Mr Shaw peered over the top of his glasses. 'Well, I have said time and time again, we need to investigate more.'

Miss White nodded her approval. 'Yes, we need to know. Otherwise…'

'Otherwise,' Mr Shaw replied. 'We both know what could happen to Middleton High, don't we?'

Daniel asked the ghost, 'What are they talking about?'

'Just listen, Daniel. They can neither see you nor hear you.'

Miss White looked towards Daniel. 'There are various rumours going around about Daniel Brady.'

'Ah!' Daniel said, hesitantly. 'She just noticed me.'

'No,' replied the ghost. 'She cannot see you.'

'I thought she did.' Daniel touched his body. 'Am I invisible?'

The ghost smiled then nodded.

Mr Shaw took Miss White's hand. 'Middleton High will have some real problems if we're not careful. We should be more vigilant. We must remain on the lookout.'

Daniel bowed his head. 'I hope they don't think I'm a troublemaker.'

Mr Shaw sat upright and gazed out of the window. 'Daniel Brady did tell me Billy Riley threw a snowball at him, and that someone got his coat wet, but Billy Riley denied it.'

Suddenly, a thud interrupted the conversation. It came from the window. They all heard it. A slushy ball of snow slid down the glass. Mr Shaw stood up. 'What in the devil's name? Who did that?'

'That made me jump,' Daniel said.

*Thud!* A second snowball hit the top corner of the window. Mr Shaw rushed to the window. A small crack appeared in the glass and began to creep diagonally across the window. Without warning, the light outside began to fade and dreary grey storm clouds appeared in the sky.

Daniel held on to the back of the couch. 'Why is it getting so dark outside? I don't like this.'

Mr Shaw backed hastily away from the window as day turned mysteriously into dusk and the heavens opened. Snowflakes fell from the sky, growing thicker and thicker by the second. Everything was rapidly changing. Snowballs as big as footballs rained down, hitting the ground with tremendous force and splashing into cascading fountains of white. Torrents of snow rebounded onto the window and began to slide down the glass in a stream of slush.

Mr Shaw called out, 'It's those evil ones.'

Daniel looked at the ghost. 'Does he mean you?'

But no answer came.

The snowstorm raged on and the wind howled outside, until a small colourful rainbow gradually became visible. It crept over the glass, slowly working its way across the window, pushing the storm to one side. Through one half of the window they saw a clear blue sky, and in the other half a violent storm still raged. The rainbow grew brighter, pushing the storm further away.

'Wicked,' Daniel said. 'That's good pushing against the forces of evil.'

Rays of light flashed across the glass. A magnificently coloured arc now spread completely across the sky and the cracked glass began to mend.

'Wow, that's the biggest rainbow I've ever seen.'

Mr Shaw sat back in his chair and wiped his forehead. 'That must be a sign they're coming. We've got to be vigilant.'

Daniel turned to the ghost. 'What do they mean?'

For the next few seconds there was an eerie silence except for the ticking of the grandfather clock: *tick-tock, tick-tock.*

The ghost took Daniel's hand. 'This is the beginning of a special journey for you, but a nasty one for others. Let us hope they learn their lesson soon, before it is too late.'

Gradually, the room began to vanish. Daniel didn't want the ghost to go. 'Wait! You said you were a ghost and my buddy, but you're also magic – so … I'm going to call you Buddy Wizard.'

# Chapter 6

It was morning. Mrs Brady popped her head around Daniel's bedroom door.

'Time to get up!'

Daniel opened his eyes. 'Where am I?'

'You're in bed, Daniel, where do you think you are?' His mum closed his bedroom door and Daniel rolled over.

'I had a nightmare, Chip.'

The little dog jumped on the bed, his ears pricked. Daniel sat up, rubbing his eyes. 'A big ghost got Riley, and I dreamed about Mr Shaw and Miss White … and Buddy Wizard. Weird.' Daniel stroked Chip. 'Did I say Buddy Wizard? I must have been dreaming.'

Daniel arrived a bit happier for the first lesson of the day, and Miss White noticed too.

'You're in a brighter mood this morning, Daniel,' she said cheerfully. 'Did something good happen last night?'

Daniel blushed and sat down, replying sheepishly, 'No, Miss.'

A few girls giggled. Daniel sank further in his chair, wishing they would all go away. He sat quietly ignoring everyone and raised the lid of his desk. 'What the—' he yelled. 'There's a dead rat in my desk – look!' All heads turned to Daniel as he dangled a big rodent by its tail. Several girls screamed.

'Drop that this instant!' shrieked Miss White. 'Where did that come from?'

Daniel quickly dropped the rat inside the desk and slammed the lid. 'I don't know, but there's another one in the classroom.'

'Where?' asked Miss White, clutching at her chest.

'It's in human form, Miss, and a lot sneakier.'

'Could you put that thing in the dustbin, *now,* please?'

The whole class looked on as Daniel left the classroom carrying the rat at arm's length. Miss White then rushed to the door. 'And don't forget to wash your hands.'

At break-time Daniel ambled despairingly along the corridor muttering, 'Riley's the rat – Riley's the rat.'

'Hi man,' came a greeting.

'Hi,' Daniel replied, uninterested, looking at the boy. He only knew him slightly.

'I saw Riley pick on you, Danny, and he threw your trainers up in the tree.'

'My name's not Danny; it's Daniel.'

'My name's Tyler, but my brother calls me Ty.'

Daniel went to shake his hand and Tyler slapped it. 'Yeah, man, gimme five.'

'Five what?' Daniel asked.

Tyler kept a straight face. 'I don't know. My older brother always says that.'

'I wish I had an older brother – to get Riley.'

Tyler pushed his glasses up his nose. 'Don't know about that. Someone picked on me once and my brother didn't do anything.'

Daniel was suddenly conscious of the noisy playground and the other pupils milling around. 'That reminds me,' he said. 'I promised to meet Sophie. Do you want to come with me?'

Tyler nodded and they ran to meet her.

Hi Sophie, this is Tyler; he wants to hang out with us.'

'Hi, Tyler,' said Sophie, holding out her hand. Tyler slapped it.

He then cheerfully added, 'Stay cool.'

'Ah, okay,' Sophie replied, her eyes flashing back to Daniel. 'Am I glad to see you! The Geeks were staring at me.' She gestured, subtly. 'They're over there, by the wall. Shall we go? I don't want to cause any more trouble.'

Daniel glanced across the playground. 'They're with Riley, so let's get out of here.'

All three sauntered away, but Tyler began to walk quicker. Side by side they strode, faster and faster. Tyler, the tallest, next to Daniel, then Sophie, who struggled to keep up with them.

'Wait, Tyler,' Daniel whispered. 'We're in the clear.'

Tyler looked behind and slowed down. 'Okay, I'm not scared.'

'Yeah,' remarked Sophie. 'So why have you got that look? They make me scared.'

'Wait,' Daniel insisted. 'We need to stick together.'

40

Sophie paused. 'Should we form a gang?'

Tyler frowned. 'You must be joking – they'll take one look at us and laugh.'

'Thanks,' remarked Sophie solemnly.

Daniel put his arm around Sophie. 'Don't worry, we'll think of something, but in the meantime watch out.'

At afternoon break, the three met in the playground. They chatted behind the wall near the entrance to the library, discussing tactics.

'They won't see us here,' Sophie said reassuringly.

Tyler fiddled with his glasses. 'Don't kid yourself.' Suddenly, all three stared in horror at Riley and the Geeks, who hovered menacingly nearby.

'So what have we here, then?' Riley asked, smirking. 'A party? Can anyone join in?'

'Get lost,' said Daniel, without thinking. Tyler began to edge slowly back.

Sophie pulled at Daniel's jacket, whispering, 'We can't fight them.'

Riley and the Geeks moved closer.

Tyler held on to his specs. 'You wouldn't hit someone wearing glasses, would you?'

'Let's leg it,' suggested Sophie. Tyler agreed, nodding furiously.

Daniel began to edge backwards. 'Okay, let's go after three.' He then shouted, 'Three!'

With that, they sprinted for the safety of the classrooms. They clattered through the nearest door. One by one they raced through the library, scattering chairs and books. All three ran along the school corridors,

41

towards the west wing with Riley and the Geeks in hot pursuit. The pounding of their footsteps echoed through the west wing then the south wing as they ran towards the crossover link.

'Hurry! Faster, Sophie!' yelled Daniel.

She caught up and ran past Daniel as he pulled over a rubbish bin, sending it rolling across the floor. Papers and cans went reeling into the pursuing trio. Riley and the Geeks tripped and stumbled over the debris, cursing. Daniel, Sophie and Tyler kept on running, pupils diving out of their way. They ran faster and faster into the east wing corridor where Daniel suddenly stopped.

'Wait! Quick, let's hide in the storeroom.' The three of them charged through the door, closed it, and kept very still.

They waited in silence until they heard Riley and the Geeks outside, asking people where they were. Then they heard a squeaking sound coming from the door. All eyes focused on the shiny handle moving downwards. Daniel was just about to grab it when they heard another voice.

'Why are you boys hanging around the storeroom?'

'Oh no, it's Miss Tubble,' Daniel whispered. 'That's all we need! Shush, listen.'

They kept perfectly still, listening to Riley's excuses, until the voices in the corridor began to fade. Daniel carefully opened the door and peered out. 'Come on, it's all clear,' he whispered. They crept quietly outside and began walking. Then: 'There they are! Let's get 'em!'

Daniel, Tyler and Sophie didn't hang around. They

sprinted along the corridor with Riley and the Geeks chasing them. They sped into the north wing corridor and ran as fast as they could straight into the main hall, but skidded to a halt when they heard the school band playing. Then everything went quiet.

'You three – what on earth is going on?' bawled the music teacher.

Daniel glanced behind him. 'Where's Riley?'

'I'll deal with this,' said a stern voice.

'Sir,' Tyler said, catching his breath, 'we were being chased.'

Mr Shaw, curious, asked Tyler, 'Who's chasing you? I can't see anyone.'

Sophie instinctively raised her hand. 'Please, sir, it's true. Bullfrog Riley was after us – I m-m-mean, Billy Riley.'

Mr Shaw turned to Daniel. 'What's your version of events, Daniel Brady?' Daniel recognised Mr Shaw's fancy waistcoat, then thought about his dream.

'It's true, sir. Riley is a bully. He did chase us.'

'Well then,' replied Mr Shaw, 'we'd better find out. Come on, you three, follow me.'

'Got it,' Daniel said, following Mr Shaw and staring again at his waistcoat.

'Got what?' asked Sophie.

Daniel hesitated then said, 'I had a weird dream; Mr Shaw wore that same waistcoat. I hadn't seen it before. Bizarre.'

Sophie wasn't taking much notice.

Mr Shaw opened the staffroom door and instructed

them to wait. Sophie bowed her head. Tyler hesitated as Mr Shaw beckoned them into the room. He pointed to a shiny table surrounded by ten leather chairs. 'Sit there,' he commanded. The walls were painted gold, with pictures of the royal family prominently displayed. The carpet was red, and there were armchairs and small tables scattered around. A strong aroma of leather filled the room. Tyler sniggered under his breath. Sophie fidgeted. But Daniel looked around the room. This room looks familiar, he thought. He gazed at the fish tank in the centre of the long wall and another thought came to his mind.

'I know, Mr Shaw!' Daniel remembered his waistcoat. 'You were in— Oh, sorry … I meant something else.'

Mr Shaw scratched his head. 'In where?'

Daniel thought of an excuse for his outburst. 'I thought you were in the corridor when Riley chased after us, sir.'

Mr Shaw rubbed his chin, looking puzzled. 'I didn't see Riley, Daniel. But I want to find out what's happening.'

Daniel suddenly felt his chair wobble. He became scared. He gripped the table, trying to keep still. Mr Shaw sensed something was wrong. 'What's the matter, Daniel?'

'Nothing, sir, I'm just stretching my legs.' Daniel wriggled around until the movement stopped. He then looked at Tyler and Sophie, but they hadn't noticed anything. It must only have happened to him. What was going on?

# Chapter 7

Mr Shaw's home was a Tudor-style cottage situated in the west of the city: a serene area with picturesque lanes and quaint shops, yet one renowned for its history of strange occurrences – people going missing, ghost sightings, and unexplained noises. The approach to Mr Shaw's cottage was along a cobbled street. It was dimly lit, and the houses were old, with white rendering and tiny windows. They leaned across the lane, as if whispering together.

Mr Shaw paused at the foot of the staircase, holding on to the balustrade that led into the open plan lounge.

'Time for me to go to bed,' he said, yawning, but instead… He sat on the comfortable armchair next to his grandfather clock then yawned again. 'Oh dear, I'm tired tonight. It must be that school wearing me out. Too much paperwork and now all these reports about bullying. What is the world coming to?'

He sat in his cosy armchair, closed his eyes and drifted off to sleep.

A couple of hours passed. Mr Shaw remained in a deep sleep, dreaming about Middleton High. In his dream, there was a knock at his front door. He opened his weary eyes. 'Who could that possibly be at this hour?' He glanced at his clock. 'It's midnight.' The old grandfather clock gave twelve dongs as the front door sounded again: *rat-a-tat-tat.* Mr Shaw called out, 'Who's there?' But no answer came. 'Okay, okay, I'm coming,' he grumbled, tottering to the front door. He peeped through his spy hole, but no one was there. Suddenly the door unlocked itself and opened, forcing him backwards. The shocked Mr Shaw came face to face with a boy dressed in rags, surrounded by a circle of light, glowing in the cool night air. 'Who on earth are you?' he asked apprehensively.

'Thank you, sir, for letting me in,' the boy said. 'I'm a friend of Jennifer Wilson, an old pupil of yours.'

Mr Shaw scratched his chin. 'Let me think. Jennifer Wilson?'

'I'm an old friend, sir. Can I come in for a minute?'

Mr Shaw was in a daze and didn't answer. He stepped sideways as the boy ghost crossed the threshold. The front door automatically closed then locked. 'Follow me,' said the boy ghost, taking Mr Shaw's hand. 'I will lead the way.'

Then in a flash of light they disappeared.

Mr Shaw opened his eyes to see a park bench overlooking a pleasant expanse of green grass and tall trees. He spotted a familiar road sign. 'This is Greenwood Park, near my old school. What am I doing here? And where did that boy go?'

The sun shone into his eyes. He raised his hand to shield the glare and waited on the path, noticing someone walking his way.

'Do I know you?' he asked.

But the girl ignored him and sat on the bench. Mr Shaw moved closer. 'Now I remember – it's Jennifer, isn't it? What's the matter?'

Jennifer didn't answer. Instead, she covered her face with her hands and sobbed.

Concerned, Mr Shaw sat next to her. 'Can I help?'

'No one cares or believes me,' she replied. 'I've had enough of Hardy and her gang.'

Mr Shaw sat, deep in thought. 'I remember now! You spoke about this some time ago. Is she still bothering you?'

Jennifer glanced along the path. 'Oh no! Here they come.'

Mr Shaw sprang to his feet. 'I can see them. Leave this to me. I'll sort this out once and for all.'

Waiting in the middle of the path, he folded his arms and watched as a group of girls approached.

'Hold it right there, girls,' he demanded. But they took no notice and kept on coming. He held out his hands to stop them. 'Right, you girls are in trouble,' he said in a louder voice. But Hardy and her gang continued towards Mr Shaw. Soon the girls were upon him.

'Hey, what's happening?' shrieked Mr Shaw, as they all walked straight through him, heading for Jennifer.

The girls swooped on Jennifer, shouting at her and hitting her. Jennifer tried to stand up, but they pushed her back down. Mr Shaw ran after them and attempted to pull the girls away, but his hand went straight through them. He flinched in horror. They kept on attacking Jennifer, punching and kicking her.

Mr Shaw called out, 'Someone help! Please help!'

His words fell on deaf ears. One girl's rucksack went flying through the air. It struck Jennifer on the side of her face. Mr Shaw shouted, 'Leave her alone, you lot! Just you wait.' He waved his fist at the girls, shouting repeatedly until they finally ran off, leaving Jennifer crying on the ground. Mr Shaw ran towards Jennifer, but as he did so the light began to fade. An eerie mist began to drift and creep around him. He dropped to his knees, then crawled along the ground, his hands outstretched. The fog became thicker. He fumbled along the ground, trying to help Jennifer, but he couldn't see her any more.

Suddenly, the frightened Mr Shaw could see clearly, but he had no idea where he was. He gazed up at a magnificent church that rose tall against the night sky. Searchlights lit up the stone walls, casting shadows across the open grounds. Inside the church, he could hear what sounded like a large congregation singing.

'Follow me,' said a voice. The boy ghost appeared and guided him towards the stone steps that led up to a wooden arched door.

'Where are we going?' asked Mr Shaw.

As they neared the entrance to the church, the singing grew louder and louder. The ghost turned to the side of the church. 'Follow me, sir.' They proceeded along a narrow path at the side of the church.

'Where are you taking me?' groaned Mr Shaw, stretching out his hand in an attempt to touch the faint blue light that surrounded the ghost.

Together, they reached the rear of the church and the boy ghost stopped, placed his hands on his hips, and stared up at the sky. 'What a beautiful sight.' His eyes twinkled like the stars.

The ghost led Mr Shaw to a small circle of shrubs a short distance away. 'This way, please, sir.'

Mr Shaw followed, shivering. The ghost pointed to the ground. A beam of light emerged from the ghost's finger and lit up a row of words.

*Jennifer Wilson, aged 15*
*Rest in Peace.*

'Oh my God!' gasped Mr Shaw. 'It's Jennifer. Whatever happened to her?'

The ghost didn't answer. He touched Mr Shaw's hand. He and the ghost lifted gently off the ground then disappeared.

Mr Shaw found himself inside the church, standing at the rear. He listened spellbound as the vicar spoke. 'Let us now pray for Jennifer Wilson, who tragically took her own life. Her torment has long passed, but let us pray for her mother, father and younger brothers, who are all with us tonight. May the Lord seek out others in our midst who need our protection.' Mr Shaw's face turned a deathly white. A twinkling of stars emerged from the ghost's finger then the light around them faded into darkness.

'Who's there?' asked Mr Shaw, waking with a start, hearing a *rat-a-tat-tat* on his front door. *Dong – Dong*

– *Dong* sounded the grandfather clock. Three o'clock. *Rat-a-tat-tat* went the knocker again. 'Okay, I'm coming. Don't be impatient. I can hear you.' Mr Shaw shuffled to the front door but stopped on his way. 'What's going on? It's three o'clock in the morning. I've been asleep a long time. I'm not falling for that trick again.'

He crept up to the window and peeked through his curtains. To his amazement he saw a shiny object on the ground. 'I thought I dreamed about something shiny,' he whispered. 'I wonder what it could be.' He slowly opened the door then cautiously glimpsed left then right and ran outside. 'Oh, my back,' he groaned, bending down. 'I'm getting old.' He grabbed the shiny object, scurried back inside and bolted the door. He leaned back against the door. 'Now, let's see what have we here.' It was a shiny pendant. As he turned it around in his hands, an image formed in his mind. He could see back into the past – he could see what had happened to Jennifer Wilson. Shocked, he let go of the pendant and it fell to the floor. Staring apprehensively at the shiny object, he carefully picked it up, then placed it on top of his grandfather clock before stumbling upstairs to bed.

The next morning, he woke early. He sat up. *What a scary dream I had about young Jennifer. Someone knocked on my door too. The pendant – it reminded me of what happened to Jennifer. How? I don't know what's happening.*

\*\*\*

The last day of term had arrived at Middleton High, and Mr Shaw was concerned about Daniel's whereabouts. Luckily, he came across Sophie, who gave him the answer he wanted. Mr Shaw rushed to his classroom and sighed with relief. 'He's okay. Now I can get on.'

He completed his reports, gathered up his paperwork, packed his personal belongings, then looked out of the window and across the school grounds. He picked up his briefcase. 'Next term I'll get to the bottom of this bullying, if it's the last thing I do.'

# Chapter 8

The summer holidays were in full swing. His painful memories of Middleton High were fading from Daniel's mind. He began enjoying the last few weeks of summer before the start of the autumn term.

The smell of freshly cut grass filled Daniel's nostrils as he mowed his parents' front lawn. *Clink, clank.* Daniel thought the blade had hit something and stopped the mower. He rolled it backwards and saw two stones on the grass. A stone hit the mower, then bounced onto the ground. Daniel instinctively looked up. His eyes immediately drawn to the faces of Bullfrog Riley and the Slippery Geeks, peering at him over the front hedge. He shuddered.

'Get lost, you lot!' Daniel shouted.

'Or else what?' jeered Riley.

'You'll see,' replied Daniel hesitantly.

'Are you going to turn us into toads?' taunted Riley.

'You're already one,' replied Daniel loudly. Seconds later he felt a sharp pain at the side of his head. He stumbled forward, feeling dizzy, then clutched his head. He lowered his hand and saw blood on his fingers. 'You coward,' Daniel sobbed, holding his head. 'Just you wait.' Blood trickled down the side of Daniel's face as

Riley and the Geeks ran off.

Later that afternoon, Mr Brady inspected Daniel's wound. 'It's only a scratch.'

'Don't you think we should report it to the police?' asked Mum.

Mr Brady chuckled. 'No, my dear, don't be silly.'

Evening arrived. Daniel lay in bed thinking. He peered through the darkness at Chip's curled up body. 'Was Buddy Wizard a dream, Chip, or is he real?'

Chip stood up on the bed then tilted his head from side to side.

'Riley has found out where I live, Chip.'

The little dog crawled along the bed and nestled alongside Daniel. They closed their eyes and it wasn't long before they fell fast asleep.

It was a warm, humid night. All seemed quiet and peaceful in Old Furrow Way. But at midnight, a trail of white glittering stars flew across the night sky and gradually descended on the Brady household. A shadowy white image drifted silently through Daniel's bedroom window and a voice whispered, 'Wake up, Daniel. Wake up. It's me, your Buddy.'

A sleepy-eyed Daniel sat up in bed, rubbing his eyes. 'Am I dreaming?'

Chip, seeing the ghost, scurried for safety under the bed covers.

The ghost dangled a glowing trail of charms from his hand, then spoke. 'When you wake, Daniel, place this around your neck. Wear it always. Hold it firmly for protection.'

Spellbound, Daniel looked at the twinkling gems as they unravelled from the boy's hand into a long shiny chain. Daniel simply slumped back into bed, closed his eyes and went to sleep again.

The next morning, sunlight filtered into Daniel's bedroom. He stretched and yawned.

'Chip, I had a weird dream last night. What's the time?' Daniel had a brief look at his watch, then felt something scrape his side. He turned over to see what it could be. 'Ah! Help, Chip,' he said, leaping out of bed. 'It's a chain!'

Little Chip remained rigid, anticipating an intruder, ready to pounce, looking at the bedroom door.

'Buddy is magic – he's a ghost wizard. It's real, Chip – I mean, he's real. Look at this.'

Daniel held the chain closer to Chip. The little dog wagged his tail and pricked up his ears, inquisitively sniffing the chain. Daniel held the chain up to his eyes. 'Look, it has little hands with fingers and a thumb, Chip, all linked together. See how it shines.'

The silver chain mesmerised both of them as Daniel fed the links through his fingers. 'I can feel something strange in these tiny hands, Chip. A real ghost gave me this. He's called Buddy. He really is Buddy Wizard.'

Daniel put the chain around his neck and fastened the link. 'Chip, this is a wizard's bond – and our secret.' Chip's ears pricked up and he gave a small bark, as if to agree.

***

Each day, Daniel wore the chain, making sure he kept it hidden beneath his T-shirt.

'Have you got something wrong with your chest?' Mum asked. 'You keep patting it.'

'No, Mum, I'm fine. I'm just flattening my T-shirt; you didn't iron it properly.'

Daniel was becoming more confident that Buddy Wizard had been sent to help him. *Or was someone playing tricks on him?* He began spending more time reading stories in his bedroom, like *The Witch's Revenge.*

'I'm waiting to see if the chain possesses any powers,' said Daniel excitedly. Chip held out his paw. 'I've still got one problem, though. Riley and the Slippery Geeks are lurking in and around the neighbourhood and I've invited Sophie and Tyler over to my new tent in the garden. What should I do, Chip?'

Chip stood on his hind legs, resting his front paws on Daniel's knee.

'I'm sorry, Chip, I didn't mean to frighten you. Come on boy, let's go into the garden and wait for Sophie and Tyler.'

It was evening. The sun was sinking behind the branches of the tall trees, All three sat huddled together in the tent. Daniel began talking and just had to tell Sophie and Tyler about the ghost, Buddy Wizard.

'Look.' Daniel cleared his throat. 'There's someone…'

He paused, uncertain what to say. 'Listen. Our

school was built on land where a castle, a manor and an orphanage once stood. These buildings had a bad history. People were bullied, starved, tortured and even killed there. In the eighteenth century the kids at the orphanage were badly beaten and starved – not only by the teachers, but by the overseers and some of the older kids too. Apparently a curse was placed on these terrible people. I read about a prophecy; it said that the badly treated children would rise once again and invoke their revenge. I even dreamed about a ghost and saw one.'

Sophie jumped. 'What did you say?'

Daniel looked at the ground. 'I know it's hard to believe.'

'You saw a ghost?' asked Sophie, rubbing her eyes. 'I hope it doesn't come anywhere near me.'

'Nor me, man.'

Daniel fumbled to find the right words. 'I didn't really mean that … I meant more like – oh, forget it. You wouldn't believe me, anyway.'

Tyler jumped up. 'Come on, Daniel, we believe you. We all want to see Riley punished – but ghosts?'

'Let me show you my chain. The ghost told me to wear it always and hold it tightly if I'm in danger.' Daniel hesitated again. 'Look, let's forget what I said.'

'No way,' replied Tyler. 'How can we forget that, Daniel? This is scary: we'd better put some lights on. We've got candles, matches and torches.'

'Okay, so you don't believe me, you're just having a laugh.'

Two small lamps lit the inside of the tent, casting

shadows, creating a spooky atmosphere perfect for fright night stories. Tyler decided to take the lead and conjured up a couple of stories about Dracula, full of blood and gore.

Sophie changed the subject. 'My dad tells me not to listen to older boys. Don't do this, don't do that. He's so annoying sometimes. I keep telling them, I can take care of myself – but I can't handle ghosts, though. It does sound scary – even coming from you, Daniel.'

Before long, all three were jumping at the slightest noise outside.

'Shush,' Tyler said. 'Can you hear that?'

'Hear what?' Sophie asked.

'Daniel's ghost.'

'Ha, ha, very funny,' Daniel replied.

'Let's look at this sensibly,' said Tyler. 'Wizards and goblins don't exist unless you're Harry Potter or the Hobbit.'

There was a strange cry. It echoed in the night air. Tyler jumped up. 'What's that?'

Sophie edged back. 'Daniel, do something.'

Everyone froze except Chip, who ran to the tent flap, barking. Daniel scrambled after him, grabbing him by his collar. 'That's next-door's cat,' he said calmly. 'Cats make some real weird noises, don't they?'

Sophie fidgeted. 'That's a relief. This is scary.'

'Look, I didn't want to scare you two,' said Daniel. 'But Bullfrog Riley and the two Geeks know where I live. They threw stones at me when I was cutting the grass.'

'You didn't tell us,' complained Sophie.

'I just did, didn't I?'

Tyler interrupted. 'You should have told us Riley knows where you live because other kids know too. I mentioned your tent. I may have said something else but Riley wouldn't come in the garden, would he?'

'No,' said Daniel angrily. 'Because he's a coward.'

Sophie agreed then twitched her nose. 'Don't tempt fate. Anyway, my mum's coming to pick me up soon.'

Outside, the sun was setting. It felt peaceful and calm. The sky was clear, with an orange glow that stretched out from the sun.

'Listen,' said Tyler. 'Can you hear something?'

'No.'

Tyler laughed. 'Nor can I, man.'

'Stop messing around,' said Sophie. 'It's scary.'

*Crack!*

Sophie jumped. 'Who's there?'

The tent flap folded back. A face appeared, and they all jumped.

'Only me,' said Mr Brady jovially.

Chip wagged his stubby tail.

'Just thought I'd let you know – it'll be dark shortly, so you'll have to come in soon and wait for your parents.'

'Yes, Dad, okay.'

With that, the tent flap closed and Mr Brady's footsteps faded away.

'It's just like my dad to poke his nose in and spoil things.'

Tyler laughed nervously. 'I thought for a minute it

could be a ghost.'

'It's getting dark and spooky out here,' said Sophie, burying her head in her hands.

Daniel reassured them. 'Don't worry; it's really safe in here. There's three of us, and Chip, so we can tackle anyone.'

Tyler shone a torch under his chin. 'Even a ghost! Let's do some more stories.'

'No,' said Sophie. 'I think we should go indoors now – just in case.'

For the next few minutes they chatted. Suddenly, jittery Sophie spotted the tent flap moving. She looked twice, but dared not look a third time, until the flap lifted again and curiosity got the better of her. She crawled to the tent flap and peered out. She couldn't believe what she saw. She gave a little squeak.

'Help! Help!' she screamed, leaping up. 'A ghost!'

They flashed their torches at the tent opening. Chip began to bark, and Tyler dived for cover in a mad flurry of excitement. Daniel clambered to the tent flap, trying to hold Chip back.

'There's no one there,' Daniel said, poking his head outside. He shuffled back towards Tyler and Sophie, when suddenly the flap lifted again, and an old man's white face appeared. Tyler and Sophie screamed. Chip shot out of Daniel's arms and went running for the tent flap, barking. Daniel quickly followed, shouting, 'Get him, Chip! Get him!'

Chip ran into the garden, barking.

A clattering came from the garden fence, amid

several thuds and bangs as the intruders scrambled over the fence and disappeared into the night.

Daniel grabbed Chip and calmed him down as Tyler and Sophie waited nervously. 'That wasn't a ghost,' said Daniel. 'That must have been Riley wearing a mask.'

Sophie shivered. 'That's not funny.'

Daniel cuddled Chip. 'They won't come back.'

'I'm scared,' replied Sophie. 'I'm going indoors.'

'Me too,' added Tyler. 'That frightened me to death.'

'I'm going to have nightmares,' said Sophie, running her fingers through her hair. 'I don't want nightmares about ghosts. It's dark and creepy out here. I'm going to tell my mum what happened.'

'Don't think I'll bother,' said Tyler.

Daniel frowned. 'If I tell my dad, he'll just laugh and say don't be so silly.'

The three walked cautiously through the back garden to the house as a thousand stars twinkled majestically in the night sky.

# Chapter 9

Tyler lived in a semi-detached house close to the school with his parents, older brother and younger sister. That night, he lay in bed, thinking about the bullying at Middleton High. This made him recall the bully at his previous school. However, his parents had moved him to Middleton High, hopeful that he could make a new start there. He knew the terrible effects bullying could have, and wanted to forget what had happened to him, but it was difficult. Tyler couldn't help cursing bullies under his breath as he dropped off to sleep. It didn't take long before his mind was racing with horrible thoughts. Soon he was asleep, tossing and turning – and experiencing some very strange dreams.

Tyler could see a ghostly figure in his bedroom. 'Who's there?' he asked trembling.

'I am the one Daniel calls Buddy Wizard. Don't be afraid. Let's go and visit someone from your past.' The ghost beckoned Tyler from his bed.

He followed and they vanished.

The bully at Tyler's old school was sleeping peacefully when the ghost and Tyler appeared. The room was dark, with only a soft light seeping through the curtains, highlighting shadows on the walls.

'Move closer to me,' requested the ghost, standing near the bully's bed.

'No way,' responded the cautious Tyler, covering his eyes and peeping through his fingers at the outline of someone in bed.

'Do not fear; you are safe.' Buddy Wizard beckoned. Tyler stepped to the bed, squinting, not knowing why. He edged closer until he heard a movement. Suddenly, the bully stirred then rolled over in bed. Tyler panicked, tripped, then fell onto the bed. He came face to face with the bully, whose eyes popped open.

Tyler screamed in horror, pushing himself back. 'It's him!'

Bully Briggs sat bolt upright. Quickly, Buddy Wizard cast a beam of light onto Tyler's face. Seeing this, Briggs froze. He stared, his mouth agape, powerless to speak. Tyler stood gawking, his eyes fixated on Briggs, also unable to speak or move.

The glow illuminated Buddy Wizard as he spoke. 'Bully Briggs, you are now to visit the Ghost of Children Past.'

Briggs dived away, pulling the covers over his head and holding them firm. Suddenly, Tyler awoke with a start, switched on his bedside lamp then sat up in bed, feeling tense. He wiped his eyes then grabbed his mobile. 'It's one in the morning. I just had the strangest dream.' He switched off the light and lay back down, thinking about telling Daniel. 'That felt real.'

It wasn't long before Tyler was fast asleep again. Once more, he started to dream of Bully Briggs and

Buddy Wizard.

Tyler's dream took him into his old school playground where he had always tried to avoid Briggs and the other bullies, but somehow they managed to find him.

'There's Tyler – yuck.'

'He's smelly.'

'Dope, more like it.'

Tyler's mind drifted once again to Daniel's ghost, wishing Buddy Wizard could bring them to justice.

'Let's go and visit Briggs again,' responded a voice in Tyler's dream.

Tyler found himself standing in Briggs' bedroom once more, Buddy Wizard at his side. A thick, radiant mist began to swirl around the dark room. A large shadow appeared, then out of the mist shuffled a tall monster in a black hooded cloak. He had a skull-like face. The light penetrated into Briggs' eyes. He woke up, then opened his eyes and peeked over the top of the covers.

The fierce ghost towered over the bed, peering down at Briggs. The ghost roared and laughed. 'Bullies, beware – I have come to give you a scare.'

Briggs leaped from the bed and in a flash the bedroom vanished.

'Where are we?' asked Tyler, looking at rows of old houses.

'We are visiting London. This is the plague of death that is written in your scriptures. Your bully will visit here, and we will judge his compassion towards these poor unfortunate souls.'

'The plague must have been really horrible,' replied

Tyler. 'I remember a history lesson about ships coming here in May 1665. The plague was spread by blood-sucking fleas that lived on black rats. It spread in London because of rubbish thrown into the streets. The rotting piles helped rats multiply. Thinking that stray dogs and cats spread the disease, the Mayor of London ordered them to be destroyed. But this only caused more deaths, because there were no dogs or cats left to kill the rats.'

'That's right. People known as searchers were paid tuppence a day to try to find out what caused the plague. When a person died of the plague, a red cross was painted on their door and the dead were nailed up inside the house. All the family members had to stay there, to try to keep the plague confined. Only doctors or searchers could enter or leave these homes.

'At night, there were shouts of "Bring out yer dead!" Soon all the churchyards were full, so pits were dug to bury the bodies in. The cold winter ended the plague in February 1666. I remember the Great Fire of London was also that year.'

'Man, I'm glad I'm not going there. Hold it! You said we were in London,' Tyler protested.

'Have no fear, Tyler – the plague is for Briggs' eyes only. There are many bullies who must change their ways. This could be a punishing test to witness children suffering.'

Tyler's eyes flashed along a narrow road lined by old buildings with signs hanging above their entrances: *WORKHOUSE.* He saw a sign – *SPIKE HOUSE* – that swayed in the wind.

Hesitantly, Tyler followed Buddy Wizard to the building, through the large door and inside. A long room confronted them. Tyler saw rows of ragged boys and girls sitting on the floor, thick long ropes trailing through their hands. Each child held a small metal pick or spike. They hacked and pulled at the rope, trying to unhook the heavy cord into thin strands.

I remember this from history, thought Tyler. This twine would be used to help keep the hulls of ships watertight.

Tyler's eyes scanned the room. He saw Bully Briggs perched on a pile of rope. Briggs sat, pale-faced, his shoulders hunched, shivering and staring at the children's disfigured, bleeding hands. The black hooded ghost hovered above Briggs, highlighting the line of dishevelled children, forcing him to look at their gaunt faces.

In front of each child stood a large sack where they had to stuff their strands of twine. Briggs heard the overseer continually reminding the children: 'Don't forget, you scallywags, you live here now. You need to earn your keep – and if you want supper, fill your sack to the brim.'

Briggs sat aghast, his mouth open, peeking at the hooded ghost.

'You will stay here,' the ghost went on, laughing, 'to witness more and visit the Stone and Bone establishments.'

Time rolled on. Bully Briggs now stared at rows of beds on the floor. They were made of straw covered in sacking. Children slept four to a bed in a dimly lit dormitory. Others cried themselves to sleep. Tiny candles flickered in the cold night air. Finally the long room fell silent.

Tyler entered another workhouse, named Stone House. He saw Briggs cowering in a dull room with a high ceiling. Boulders were heaped up along one side of the room. Men laboured, striking the stone with sledgehammers, cracking the boulders into large stones. On the other side of the room teenage boys were using small hammers to break the stones into smaller pieces, then shovelling the rubble into sacks. The boys' hands looked sore and frail. They coughed to rid their throats of the dust. Dust particles floated around, clinging to everyone's clothes and settling on their hands and faces.

'Come over 'ere, Briggs,' a man barked. 'Sit down and start smashing 'em smaller. These stones are going in our new roads. You'll maybe get fed tonight, if you're lucky.'

Briggs nodded worriedly then turned to comfort the scrawny boy sobbing next to him. The hooded ghost drifted near to Briggs to listen and judge his compassion.

'This is an awful place,' remarked Tyler.

Buddy Wizard looked at Tyler. 'Your bully has one more visit to go.' Buddy Wizard took Tyler's hand and they vanished again.

They stood outside a place that Tyler thought was another factory, only this time the sign outside read *BONE HOUSE*. He sensed the grim atmosphere as they entered the building. At one end of the room he saw bones everywhere – in large baskets, on shelves, some scattered across the floor. Bones of all shapes and sizes were piled high.

Men, women and children sat on the floor in rows. All looked pale and undernourished. Each held some sort of hammer, which they used to strike the bones and break them into small fragments. Tyler's eyes flashed to Bully Briggs who sat with the children, some of whom struggled to lift the hammer. Many had cuts where fragments of sharp bone had cut their skin.

'Come on, you lot,' ordered a man. 'Keep smashing them into bits – the smaller the better. You'll get the hang of making these old animal bones into fertiliser to help our harvest grow.'

Tyler watched. He remembered this from history too. He recalled that the workhouses were more like prisons, where poor people were treated terribly and most became sick and died young. He watched as Briggs cuddled a young girl, took her hammer, and began breaking the bones for her. The hooded ghost stood nearby, peeking at Briggs with sunken eyes. Back and forth he paced until he glared at Briggs and said, 'It would appear you have compassion.'

Bully Briggs looked up at the ghost. Then he disappeared from Tyler's mind.

Tyler woke with a start and opened his eyes to daylight streaming through his window. He suddenly thought of Bully Briggs.

*What a strange dream. Ghosts, compassion – that wasn't the Briggs I knew. He had no sympathy.*

'I gotta tell Daniel about this dream.'

# Chapter 10

Dawn broke. The sun's rays glistened through the cluster of branches that hovered over Daniel's tent. Shadows stretched out over the lawn and leaves rustled in the breeze. The garden was alive with birds chirping, and bright flowers. It was Sunday. The following day was the first day of September, and the start of a new school year.

Daniel's mum continued with the household chores. Dad tended to the garden and the car but, like most children, Daniel tried to avoid doing any chores – unless, of course, money was on offer.

Daniel cuddled Chip, thinking about school and how he might be in the same class this year as Sophie and Tyler.

The next day, Daniel arrived, mildly apprehensive into the playground of Middleton High. Nothing much had changed, apart from an influx of new Year 7s. He glanced around, checking out the new arrivals. *They're a lot smaller than I am. I wonder if Riley will pick on one of them instead of me.*

In Daniel's first lesson, Miss White smiled at him. 'How is your sister getting along since leaving school?'

Daniel smiled back at Miss White, thinking, shut up.

You're always embarrassing me.

'Okay, Miss, she's getting on fine,' replied Daniel, fiddling with his chain and looking around for Riley. *Why is she giving me lots of attention?* he thought. *Perhaps my chain has special powers to influence people.*

The morning wore on. Daniel ambled from classroom to classroom. To his delight Tyler and Sophie were in his classes. He kept looking around for Riley and the Geeks, but couldn't see them.

Lunchtime arrived and Daniel sat in the school canteen, along with Tyler and Sophie. Several rows of tables and chairs lined the large hall, with dozens of pupils eating and chatting amid a clatter of dishes and cutlery.

'There you are, Daniel Brady,' said Mr Shaw. 'Sorry if I startled you, lad. I didn't mean to creep up on you. How was your summer break?'

Daniel coughed. 'Fine, thank you, sir.'

Mr Shaw stroked his moustache. 'Regarding the meeting we had last term, I have completed my report and it's gone to Mr North, the head teacher.'

Daniel held his breath, surprised. 'Thank you, sir.'

Mr Shaw turned to walk away, then hesitated. 'In the meantime, let me know if you have any more trouble with Riley. I want to know everything that happens in this school. Our anti-bullying policy needs revising.'

'That's wicked,' cheered Sophie. 'Riley's in trouble.'

Tyler slurped his soup. 'Cool, man. I wouldn't want to be in his shoes. Mr Shaw's probably looking for him right now.'

Daniel laughed but then felt his chair being jerked back. He glanced over his shoulder. To his horror, Bullfrog Riley stared back at him, looking very angry. The Geeks remained next to him, looking equally nasty. Riley poked Daniel in the back.

'Who told Shaw I picked on you?'

Daniel nervously held on to his chain and stuttered, 'N-n-not me.'

'You're in for it,' Riley sneered, pushing his face closer. He glared into Daniel's eyes then studied his chain more closely. The chain glittered and emitted a red glow, which streamed into Riley's eyes.

Daniel dared not move. He saw Riley's eyes turn orange, then red. Daniel panicked. He screamed and pushed his chair sideways, trying to escape. His chair fell to the floor, hitting Sophie on the way down.

Riley laughed then gazed at Sophie and Tyler, revealing to them his piercing red eyes.

'Arghh!' shrieked Sophie, tipping and sliding off her chair.

'Shove off!' Tyler said, panicking and tripping over Daniel trying to get away.

Riley laughed then looked at the Geeks. They gasped and stumbled backwards. Mary Simmons, a new girl, caught a glimpse of Riley's fiendish eyes. She ran, screaming, out of the canteen.

The canteen had fallen silent, apart from the sound of a dinner plate smashing on the floor. Everyone stared at Riley. He slumped on the table holding his forehead. Miss Tubble charged through the canteen.

'What's going on here, Daniel Brady?' she bawled. 'What are you doing on the floor? Get up at once – you're on report.'

Miss Tubble then proceeded to Riley, her hands on her hips. 'What's the matter, Billy?' she asked sympathetically.

Riley wiped his forehead and eyes. 'It's Brady, Miss, it's Brady – he's the troublemaker.'

'What has he done this time?'

'Quick, let's get out of here,' Tyler suggested.

'Yes,' agreed Sophie. 'Riley seems normal now.'

'He'll never be normal,' responded Daniel. 'Let's go.'

All three slithered along the floor then darted out of the canteen.

That afternoon, Daniel, Tyler and Sophie met in the science room. Daniel flicked through the pages of a book. 'Red eyes – there's nothing about red eyes in here.'

Sophie waited near a skeleton. 'It's a bit weird standing near this thing. It's looking at us. Can't we go to the library instead?'

Daniel rocked the skeleton. 'Smart move. He's rattled, anyway. Come on.'

They crept out into the corridor. They had agreed, no matter what, that they would stick together.

'You three,' shouted a harsh voice. 'What are you doing inside?'

They stopped.

71

Daniel whispered, 'Look out – it's Griffin.'

'I said, what are you three doing inside?' Miss Griffin asked loudly. 'And don't give me any backchat. I eat kids like you for breakfast.'

Sophie nudged Daniel. 'Let's go, quick.' Tyler had the same idea and began to walk. Then all three ran as fast as they could, through the corridors, out on to the busy playground, stopping only to hide behind other boys and girls.

'We're in trouble now,' said Daniel. 'Griffin takes us for history.'

Sophie sighed. 'The witch will get us.'

'It won't be long,' added Tyler. 'We can't escape.'

'She can't either,' said Daniel. 'I think the ghost will get her.'

Daniel held out a clenched fist and Sophie and Tyler did the same. Then they touched knuckles to signal their agreement.

The few days that followed went by without Billy Riley, who had apparently gone home after the canteen incident. Riley's sudden eye complaint became a topic for discussion throughout Year 8.

\*\*\*

It was Friday – and Miss Tubble's maths lesson. Daniel, Sophie and Tyler sat together looking at her as she wrote algebra equations on the board.

Sophie twiddled with her pen and asked, 'Did Riley's eyes really turn red in the canteen?'

'Yeah, definitely,' replied Daniel. 'Just like Tubble's face when she's angry.'

Suddenly Miss Tubble spun round.

*'Brady!'* She beckoned. 'Come out here and do this sum.'

Daniel stood up and went sheepishly to the front of the class. He took the pen Miss Tubble gave him, and looked questioningly at the whiteboard. This is difficult, he thought, looking at the sum before attempting it.

'Come on, Brady, we haven't got all day.'

Daniel tried to work his way through the sum, but had to keep stopping to rub out his calculations.

'Come on, Brady,' taunted Miss Tubble. 'What's the next part, then?'

Daniel eventually bowed his head. 'I'm not sure, Miss.'

'Oh, sit down, Brady! You're too slow. Let someone a bit smarter take over.'

A few girls giggled. Daniel felt a surge of heat come to his face. He knew his face was glowing red as he slunk back to his desk and sat down. He began to fiddle with his chain, glaring at Miss Tubble, wondering how he could get his own back on her and turn her into something.

Daniel glanced outside as it began to rain. He watched the droplets bounce off the playground, splash and burst into steam. The water swished along the window frame. Daniel became mesmerised by the noise as it grew louder and louder.

*'Brady, pay attention!'* demanded Miss Tubble.

Daniel jumped, along with several other kids. She glared at Daniel then forced a sinister smile. 'Now, where was I?'

Daniel felt relieved when break-time arrived. He moped in the playground, watching a rainbow arcing across the sky. 'Tubble is an old battle-axe.'

'She's an old goat,' added Sophie.

'More like a wrinkly old crow,' said Tyler.

Daniel kicked at a small puddle then suddenly felt a tug on the back of his collar. He lost his balance, stumbled backwards and fell to the ground. He could feel the cold water soaking through his trousers and then spotted Riley running away, laughing.

'That's it,' Daniel said. 'I'm going to find Mr Shaw.' He trudged off, his soggy clothes clinging to him, while Sophie and Tyler looked on helplessly.

Two hours later, in dry clothes, Daniel headed for Miss Griffin's history lesson with Sophie and Tyler. As expected, he felt apprehensive. When he entered the classroom, Miss Griffin forced a smile at him. She never smiles at me, thought Daniel. What's up with her?

She began the lesson by pacing the floor.

'Okay, boys and girls,' she croaked. 'Who can tell me any important event that took place in the fourteenth century?'

Several girls responded.

'The start of the Hundred Years' War, Miss.'

'The Coronation of Edward the Third, Miss.'

'Very good,' said Miss Griffin. 'Now who can name an important event that happened in the fifteenth century?'

A few hands went up, but Miss Griffin ignored these and peered astutely around the classroom until she came to Daniel.

'What about you, Brady?' she asked, staring at him. 'Can't you give me an answer?'

Daniel remained silent.

'Don't you know, Brady?' Miss Griffin waited for an answer. The other pupils sat gawking at Daniel. He gulped before answering.

'The most important event could be Joan of Arc, Miss. She was burned for being a witch.'

Tyler and Sophie sniggered. Miss Griffin didn't answer. She walked slowly away, up and down the aisles, mumbling to herself. She then turned and glared at Daniel.

'Witches date back beyond the tenth century,' she said, raising her black eyebrows. 'But do they exist today?' She paused and her eyes wandered around the room. 'Well, do they?'

Daniel muttered, 'You should know.' He couldn't help noticing her hair separating, strands lifting up in the air, curling away from her head as if electrified. *Oh no,* he thought. *What's happening? The others must be able to see her hair moving. They're pointing. Maybe she is a witch.*

Miss Griffin stared back at Daniel then snapped, 'Well, Brady, what do you think?'

'Um, about what, Miss?'

'Witches, of course, boy – what else?'

Daniel looked at Sophie, who giggled nervously. Tyler sat still. Daniel noticed other kids laughing and kept a straight face.

'Stop that laughing, or else!' shouted Miss Griffin striding briskly to Daniel's seat. 'And you, Brady, will soon be on report.'

Daniel sat miserably through Grumpy Griffin's lesson, and was glad when it ended – along with the first week of school.

The three walked out of Griffin's classroom, Daniel mimicking Griffin's long, crinkly finger. He pointed back at her and whispered: 'Witch of the east, witch of the west, get on your broomstick and give it a rest.'

Sophie and Tyler dashed past Daniel.

'Yeah, fly away, witch, fly away!' said Sophie.

# Chapter 11

Lots of kids chatted eagerly afterwards about what had happened to Miss Griffin's hair – and how. Daniel smiled, knowing it could only be due to static electricity. He lay in bed listening to thunder rumbling in the distance. Long spells of silence allowed him to drift off to sleep, but every time the thunder crashed he woke. Then there was an almighty *crack*. The bedroom lit up. There was a boom. The sky shook with flashes and bangs as a fierce storm raged over Old Furrow Way.

Daniel tapped his hand on the bed covers. 'Chip – here, boy.' The trembling little dog readily obliged. 'The storm's really close, Chip. Shall we take a look?' He held Chip tightly, stepped out of bed and walked over to the window. Inquisitively, he pulled back the curtain. They saw a jagged streak of lightning hit a tree. The ground lit up.

'Wow,' said Daniel. 'Did you see that, Chip? Look! It's on fire.' But Chip wasn't looking; he had buried his head in Daniel's arms.

Sparks flickered from the base of the tree, and bright lights surged through the sky. Daniel shivered. He whispered to Chip, 'Come on, boy, let's get back to bed.' They snuggled together under the covers and Daniel dropped off into a deep sleep.

It didn't take long before Daniel was dreaming of seeking revenge on anyone who had picked on him or had been nasty to him recently. In his dreams, a ghost appeared in his bedroom.

'Wicked! It's him, Chip,' said Daniel. 'I knew he could be real.'

Chip gave a small bark to agree.

'Sorry, Daniel,' said the ghost boy, brushing the dust from his clothes. 'I didn't mean to frighten you; I was caught up in a thunder bolt.'

Daniel became spellbound by the tiny stars that twinkled all around the shabby ghost.

'I'm here,' said Daniel, wriggling out from under the bed.

'Come, Master Daniel,' said the boy ghost. 'You are required to journey with me.'

'Where are we going?'

'Fear not. You will see.'

A small ray of light shot out from the ghost's finger and across the room, hitting Daniel. Chip leaped onto the bed then jumped into Daniel's arms. All three of them disappeared.

'Where are we?' asked Daniel, glancing around a shadowy room that was lit only by streetlights shining through a window onto a row of books. 'Is this some sort of library? It looks scary.'

They could hear a swishing noise. Slowly, a ghostly figure emerged from the darkness. The frightened Daniel moved instinctively away. Then he breathed a sigh of relief seeing Sophie, wearing a white nightdress.

'Sophie,' said the startled Daniel, 'how did you get here?'

'Do you mean, how did *we* get here?' asked Tyler, appearing next to her.

The three stood staring at each other. Chip wagged his tail as Sophie stroked him. 'Are you scared, Chip? I'm petrified.'

Tyler shivered and looked suspiciously around. 'Where are we? I want to go home.'

Sophie cuddled Chip 'We're in a weird place. Please, let's go.'

'It's Buddy Wizard! Don't be scared. I told you he was real.'

Their eyes adjusted to the dark and they could vaguely make out a bookcase, a table, chairs and ornaments. Daniel felt for a light switch. 'Let's see if we can throw some light on this place.' *Click.* 'It doesn't work.' He reached up to a small shelf unit near the window. 'I can feel … Yuk, cigarettes.'

He wiped his hands on his pyjamas. 'I can feel a pen,' he said, putting it back. 'What's this? Oh, a candle. And what's this?' He picked up a lighter, lit it and then lit the candle.

The candle illuminated a shadowy room with a staircase in one corner.

'I wonder where that leads,' said Sophie, edging backwards.

'We'll find out,' Daniel replied. 'I'll hold Chip now. You take the candle.'

'Why?' she asked.

'So you can lead the way upstairs.'

'Why?' she asked, as Daniel took hold of Chip.

'Because you're the shortest,' explained Daniel, passing her the candle.

The dog trembled as Sophie reluctantly led the way up the long, winding staircase, holding the candle. The flame flickered, casting shadows that stretched with every movement. Up they went, climbing cautiously together, feeling their way along. At the top, Sophie lifted the candle higher, revealing a shadowy hallway.

Daniel pointed then whispered, 'Go that way.'

They crept to a partly open door. Carefully, Sophie nudged it open. She hesitated for a moment. Daniel prodded her. 'Go on,' he said. 'It's okay, we're behind you.'

Sophie ventured in, holding the candle.

'What's that smell?' asked Daniel, sniffing. 'Galloping ghouls, I know that smell.'

All three remained motionless, staring at the outline of a bed. They could see faint strands of long black hair trailing over a pillow. They heard a snore. Suddenly, there was movement and someone in the bed sat bolt upright.

'Who's there?' croaked a female voice.

'I-i-it's Griffin,' Sophie squeaked, trembling. She panicked. Turning quickly, she accidentally lit up the faces of Daniel and Tyler with the flame of the candle. Miss Griffin screamed: a piercing noise that shot through the air. Tyler leaped back and cracked his head on the door. He yelped.

'Who's there?' shrieked Miss Griffin again.

Daniel whispered. 'Shush – be quiet. Make out we're ghosts.'

Tyler furiously rubbed his head. 'That hurt.'

Daniel took the candle and pushed it forward. Miss Griffin grabbed the bed covers and pulled them over her head. Daniel then hummed in a deep voice.

Sophie, however, was staring at something else. 'Look,' she whispered. 'Cat's eyes.' Suddenly, a black cat hissed and leaped past them. Chip jumped out of Daniel's arms and chased after it, barking. The three ran out of the room then stopped, bumping into each other.

'Where did Chip go?' asked Daniel, holding the candle higher. They could just see Chip's tail going through a doorway. Daniel darted after him. 'Here, boy,' he whispered, pushing the door open.

Sophie stayed close behind, panicking. 'We've got to get out of here,' she said. 'Let's go.'

Tyler stepped hastily away. 'I agree.'

'Shut up, you two,' snapped Daniel. 'I've got to get Chip.'

Fearfully, Sophie hesitated and edged away. 'What's that?' she whispered.

A wrinkly old lady sat up in bed, staring at them with dark eyes. 'Who's there?' she asked warily. Her piercing voice made Chip howl and the cat arched its back, hissing. 'Shoo, shoo,' she yelled, picking up a vase full of flowers and hurling it at Chip, forcing him to jump out of the way. The vase hit the bedroom door, narrowly missing Daniel.

The old lady threw back the covers, slowly got out

of bed and tottered towards them. The candle showed the giant shadows of a cat and dog stretched across the wall behind her.

Daniel, Sophie and Tyler turned tail and ran, heading for the stairs. The cat streaked past them, Chip in hot pursuit. Daniel blew out the candle as they thumped down the stairs, then the lights in the house suddenly came on.

'Stand still,' the boy ghost commanded. Daniel, Sophie and Tyler stopped like statues at the foot of the stairs. The ghost ushered them away. 'Go and stand over there.'

Daniel, Sophie and Tyler seemed to be mesmerised. They tiptoed silently where he pointed. On the wall hung two broomsticks alongside a display of brass ornaments. Just then, there were heavy footsteps.

'Wake up,' said Daniel to Tyler and Sophie.

Sophie and Tyler suddenly snapped out of their trance. To their dread they saw Miss Griffin, dressed in a horrid black nightgown, walk down the stairs.

'Oh, no, we're in for it now.' Sophie gulped, hiding behind Tyler.

'Get us out of here,' Tyler pleaded, stepping back and treading on Sophie's foot.

'Ouch!' yelped Sophie.

Daniel put his hand over her mouth. 'What's the matter with you two?' he whispered. 'She's only a bit of a witch – we've got a real Buddy Wizard to protect us.'

Daniel checked out the black cat, sitting on the floor licking itself. Chip lay nearby, growling. Miss Griffin stooped and picked up the cat.

'I had a nightmare, Wilfred,' she said, cuddling the

cat. 'I thought I saw a ghost and heard a dog barking.' She chuckled. 'Silly thing.'

Suddenly, she heard a noise. A broomstick lifted from the wall, moving towards her. The three stood, captivated, their eyes glued to the broomstick snaking towards Miss Griffin. She screamed. 'Get away! Help!' She panicked, dropping the cat, then the broomstick pinned her to the wall. The children stood, agog, as the boy ghost controlled the broomstick with his finger.

'What's going on down there?' called a croaky voice from upstairs.

'Nothing, Mother – just w-w-wait,' Miss Griffin called out, grappling with the broomstick. 'What on earth is happening to me? Please stop,' she screamed, her face grey with shock and her body trembling.

Sophie spoke, concerned. 'That's cruel, Daniel.'

'I agree. She's not a real bully, just a bit too strict. The ghost should know.'

'Here comes Griffin's mum,' Sophie whispered nervously, looking up at the old lady, who shuffled down the stairs.

The old lady leaned over the staircase then reached out with her craggy hand, trying to touch Tyler's head. 'I can hear someone! Who's there?' she squeaked.

Tyler ducked and closed his eyes.

Miss Griffin lay on the floor, petrified, holding the handle of the broomstick, her nightgown entwined in the long twigs. Her face was sheened in sweat.

'I feel faint. Thank goodness that's stopped,' she groaned, struggling to her feet. 'I'm coming, Mother. Go back to bed.'

The three kept perfectly still, waiting for her to go back upstairs. Chip lay under a small table, only venturing out when Miss Griffin picked up the cat. 'I don't want all the children to think I'm a witch, do I, Wilfred?' she said. 'I'm not a witch, am I, Wilfred?'

Daniel watched as the boy ghost thrust his finger at Miss Griffin. A small ball of light flew across the room, then a twinkling star dropped into her hair.

Buddy Wizard smiled at Daniel. 'I think your teachers may soon see the error of their ways.' Gradually, the light faded and the room vanished.

'Thank God that's over,' said Daniel.

Back in his own bed, Daniel sat bolt upright and opened his eyes. 'It's morning, Chip! That was a crazy dream. I dreamed I went to Griffin's house with Buddy Wizard, Sophie and Tyler. You were there too.'

The dog jumped up on the bed, vigorously wagging his stubby tail. 'Quick, Chip, we've got to speak to Sophie and Tyler. What day is it?' Daniel jumped out of bed.

'Woah, slow down! Where are you going?' asked Mr Brady, walking upstairs.

'Sorry, Dad, I've got to speak to Sophie.' Daniel jumped the last few steps of the staircase then grabbed his mobile. Daniel tapped his fingers until he heard Sophie's voice.

'Sophie, listen. I had a weird dream last night. I was in Griffin's house with you and—' Daniel stopped talking and listened to Sophie. 'It happened to you too? So now do you believe me?'

# Chapter 12

That evening Daniel, Sophie and Tyler met in Daniel's bedroom. 'Do you believe me now about Buddy Wizard?'

'Sort of,' replied Tyler. 'I had a crazy dream about the bully at my other school. Last night we went to Griffin's house. In the past few weeks I've dreamed some weird things – and been picked on at school. Boy, I'm so glad it's easy to forget dreams.'

'I've had strange dreams too, because of all your talk about ghosts. I daren't tell my parents what we talk about, Daniel. You said your theories come from your books, but they're not true, are they?'

Daniel shrugged his shoulders. 'You don't have to believe me.'

Tyler picked up *Ancient Spells* and flicked to the page that Daniel had spoken about. 'Let's have a look about the orphanage. It's interesting about Middleton Manor – a prophecy, magicians and ghosts. Why do you think it has anything to do with our school?'

'The name in the book says Middleton Castle and Middleton Manor. Our school is called Middleton High. The tree I climbed must have been originally planted in the grounds of the castle and manor. There was a message from the past etched on the tree. You said the school plaque suddenly shone after I rubbed it, Sophie. The chain left on my bed, that's real!'

'I'm not sure about that tree – we didn't see the wording appear,' argued Sophie. 'Let's test your chain theory.'

'Okay then,' replied Daniel. He rubbed the chain, but nothing happened. He manipulated the chain, rolled it between his fingers, but still nothing happened. 'I'm not in any danger, so maybe it won't work. Could you two help? Let's try this together.' Daniel unhooked the chain and held it up. Tyler and Sophie touched it – then they heard a crash and the curtains lifted.

Sophie nearly jumped out of her skin. 'What was that?' she asked.

'That's the wind,' replied Daniel, looking at the mess on the floor. 'The window flew open and blew the curtains. Oh no, Mum will kill me – it's smashed a photo.' He hurriedly cleared up the mess, hoping his parents wouldn't notice. 'But I think the chain does have powers,' Daniel continued. 'Look what happened to Riley.'

'Daniel's right,' said Tyler. 'Look what happened in the school canteen.'

Sophie peered under the bed. 'If my mum only knew what's been happening she would definitely ground me.'

Daniel kept a straight face. 'The dream I had about Miss Griffin's home was real scary and you two were in it … It just seemed so real.' He pointed up to the ceiling and spelled out a word with his finger. 'I'm spelling

Tubble. I wish someone would teach the bully Tubble a lesson. In fact, I think all nasty teachers should be taught a lesson.'

'I do too,' agreed Sophie, stretching to the floor, looking under the bed again. 'I think I'll stay awake tonight – just in case.'

Tyler laughed. 'In case what?'

'In case a ghost visits,' said Daniel.

Sophie edged away. 'That's not funny, Daniel.'

Then the bedroom door opened suddenly and a head appeared.

She jumped.

'Come on, you two, your parents are here,' said Mr Brady.

Later that evening, Sophie was at home in bed, snuggling up to her teddy bear. She daren't tell her parents about Daniel's ghost because she thought they would want her to stay away from him. She thought about all the horrible teachers at school. Why could they be like that? Then she started to drift off to sleep.

It wasn't long before Sophie fell into a deep sleep – and began to dream about nasty teachers.

What's that strange glow? Help! I'm drifting out of bed, thought Sophie. A creepy mist surrounded her. She stood in a brightly lit hall, Daniel and Tyler by her side.

All three gazed up at the huge domed ceiling. The room contained tiered rows of seats. The children stood at the bottom row of seats, in their pyjamas. Sophie observed strange objects scattered across the floor in front of them, and beyond trailed a long red curtain spanning the hall.

Tyler nosed around. 'Look at that cannon.'

'Where are we?' asked Sophie.

'I don't know,' replied Daniel. 'Looks like a sort of observatory with that high ceiling.'

'We're dreaming, aren't we?' Tyler asked.

'Your ghost must have done this,' claimed Sophie.

'Buddy Wizard may come – he told me to expect some surprises. Perhaps this is one of them. Look over there.'

Men and women began to file into the hall. They headed up the aisles then sat in the rows of seats. The hall was rapidly filling up.

Tyler noticed a man with a goatee. 'He looks just like the geography teacher from school.'

'There are no other children in here,' remarked Sophie. 'I don't like this.'

Daniel tried to reassure her. 'Try not to be scared,' he whispered.

'Good evening, ladies and gentlemen,' came a voice.

'It's Buddy Wizard,' Daniel said excitedly. 'I recognise his voice. Look! There he is.'

They looked up at a raised platform twenty metres away. Beneath the platform stood a red magnet two metres high.

'Let's go over there,' suggested Daniel.

'I represent all school pupils,' boomed the ghost. 'And I welcome you to this year's lesson on bullying – for teachers.'

'This is a strange lesson,' said Sophie.

'That's good – some teachers need a lesson,' Daniel said.

The air around the ghost glowed and he spoke again. 'Now, let us all imagine a bully teacher who picks on children.'

An angry growl rumbled through the hall.

The boy ghost raised his hand. 'Yes, I know what you're thinking – children can be troublesome. Well, that's another reason why we are here today. Now let's return to my lesson, but, before I do…'

Suddenly, he detected Sophie. 'Come closer.'

Sophie looked at Daniel. 'He means us.'

Daniel led the way. 'Come on – it'll be okay.'

The three strolled through the arch of the magnet.

'The magnet's changed our clothes!'

They were now wearing their school uniform. A shroud of mist floated above them.

The ghost directed them towards other children seated nearby. 'Sit there,' he commanded. He swept his hand through the air, and a screen appeared, showing a classroom full of children with Miss Tubble standing at the whiteboard. 'We will now observe how Miss Tubble teaches.'

The audience of teachers witnessed boys and girls sitting at desks facing Miss Tubble. She stomped around the classroom for five minutes, upsetting pupils with her shouting and rudeness. Throughout the observation, some teachers cheered, to show their approval, while others booed.

'We have all seen how Miss Tubble teaches,' said the

ghost. 'Now let's see what one of you knowledgeable gentlemen can do.'

Everyone sat motionless, trying to look inconspicuous.

'You, sir,' the ghost said, pointing to a monster of a man with sleek black hair who slouched in his seat, nearly squashing two small ladies who sat either side of him.

'Yes, you at the back – you are too large to hide.'

A beam of light shone onto the man, who rose from his seat as if he had filled with air. The man hovered, face down, above the shocked audience then flew over their heads to the classroom, where he landed and fell over. The boys and girls roared with laughter. But that soon changed. The man became angry. He raged at the children, out of control, shouting at them. The audience of teachers tutted.

The ghost's voice echoed again. 'I think the boys and girls need more entertainment – do you all agree?'

All the children cheered.

'Time to return to your seat, sir,' the ghost dictated, waving his finger at the monster teacher. The boys and girls gasped as the teacher zoomed overhead and came to a halt above his seat and was then gradually lowered into it, nestling once again between the two small ladies.

The ghost proceeded along, in view of the audience then stopped.

'Luckily,' he said, 'there are only a few teachers who need further education. The more mistakes they make, the more lessons they need.' He turned to Miss Tubble, who was busy manicuring her fingernails. 'Education,' he continued, 'can occur in other ways, and I have a simple test.'

Sophie, Daniel and Tyler sat, fascinated, wondering what test would happen next.

'Miss Tubble is a bully teacher,' said Sophie. 'What's he doing with that rope tied around her leg?'

'Er, I don't know,' replied Daniel. 'She's wriggling, trying to get it off. It doesn't look good.'

Miss Tubble shot up in the air, swirling around the ghost's head. The rope tied to one leg. He swung her around like a rag doll.

'I am like earth's gravity,' the ghost explained. 'This bully teacher is moving in a circle around me. I can feel her pulling away from me, but I am holding her in this circle. Just imagine: if I was a hundred times bigger, her pull would be less and my control would be greater.' He clumsily lowered Miss Tubble to the ground amid groans from the teachers, then turned to the boys and girls.

'Now, for my next lesson,' said the ghost, 'I need two volunteers.'

Everyone shrank back in their seats.

The ghost beckoned to a small, spindly man sitting to the far right, six rows back. 'You, please, sir.'

He then pointed to a younger man with a ponytail who tried to hide. The teachers rose over the spectators' heads, landing beside Miss Tubble.

'Let us call this higher education,' the ghost said. 'Now, you three – yes, that includes you, Miss Tubble – stand closer.'

The three teachers shuffled reluctantly together. The

ghost raised his hand and they rose higher and higher until all three hung near the ceiling.

'Let's add two objects up there for good measure,' said the ghost. He hurled a cannon ball and a small marble up in the air and they hovered alongside the three teachers. 'Gravity works the same for all objects, no matter what their size,' he continued. 'Will this affect how fast they fall? The answer is possibly not. Air resistance, or the inclusion of air on, or in, an object can affect how fast it falls. But remember, gravity works in a mysterious way. Small or large objects all fall at the same speed – provided, of course, one hasn't got a parachute.'

With that all three teachers, the cannon ball and the marble dropped to the ground. The audience gasped. Sophie was amazed that everything fell at the same speed and stopped a metre from the ground, almost at the same time. The ghost turned to the boys and girls, who sat motionless, their mouths agape.

'Now do you understand?' he asked. Suddenly the teachers, the cannon ball and the marble dropped to the floor, landing with several thumps.

'Gravity and power go on throughout our universe. The sun controls the earth, which orbits around it – just like bullies try to control others. And Miss Tubble may get a different lesson – if she's not careful.'

Sophie focused on Miss Tubble, who perspired profusely. The spindly man's knees knocked together and the young man with the ponytail kept coughing, sounding like a horse.

'Let the children decide how you three will return

to your seats,' the ghost went on. 'All those in favour of seeing them walk back to their seats, thumbs up. Flying back to their seats, thumbs down.'

To the delight of Sophie, Daniel and Tyler, it was thumbs down. All three teachers rose from the ground and went back to their seats.

'Ladies and gentlemen,' the ghost continued, 'those of you who haven't learned anything yet will have further opportunities to see the error of your ways. The second part of this lesson is not suitable for children.'

Gradually, the lights dimmed and the curtains parted.

'Do we have to stay?' asked Sophie.

Daniel scratched his head. 'I thought he said this wasn't for children?'

'We'd better leave then,' said Tyler.

All the girls and boys sat at their desks, looking at the screen. Then the floor trembled and lifted the desks, two at a time. Daniel gripped his chair and flew headlong into the giant screen.

Tyler closed his eyes. 'What's going on?'

Sophie, seeing them vanish, held her desk as tightly as she could.

Then she awoke with a start, let go of the bed covers, and sat bolt upright. 'Oh my God, what a terrible dream. The ghost … and the teachers being taught a lesson … and Daniel and Tyler were there!' Sophie jumped out of bed. 'I've got to tell Daniel.'

# Chapter 13

Daniel was back in school, wary of the unpredictable Riley. He wanted to fight back but didn't know how. He pondered over the south wing plaque, Sophie at his side.

'It seemed so real last night, Daniel. I told my mum. She said, "Oh dear, I hope that school isn't scaring you." I thought, no, Mum, but Daniel is. I didn't tell her everything, though, so don't worry.'

'I'm glad you didn't. She'd probably start firing questions at me or my mum.'

'My dream took me to a very peculiar place, Daniel. It was so unusual – and a bit scary. Miss Tubble was in it, and so were you, and Tyler. There was a ghost, sort of educating and punishing teachers. I felt sorry for the teachers.'

'I know, Sophie,' replied Daniel. 'I've had strange dreams too. I reckon this is all happening because of me.'

'Have the plaques got something to do with all this?' Sophie asked. 'Why do you keep looking at them?'

'I'm certain they've helped me feel better. I think this plaque could be from the old Middleton Manor. I just want to have another look at it and write something down.'

'Okay,' Sophie said, looking cautiously around. 'I don't want to get picked on, Daniel. I'm going in case someone comes.'

*All I learn is from here, with my eyes in a book.*
*If there is darkness, I will provide you with comfort and light.*
*Your powerful dreams will inspire your noble action*
*Look to the future and forever display your great might.*

Suddenly, someone tugged at Daniel's chain from behind. 'Get off!' Daniel said, turning.

'What have we here, then?' asked Riley, pushing his face closer to the chain.

'Get off my chain, you geek,' replied Daniel, grabbing Riley's hand.

The startled Riley pulled the chain tighter. 'What did you call me?'

Daniel turned his head sideways. 'Yuck, your breath hums of onions.'

Riley looked back at the Slippery Geeks. 'Did you hear that, lads?'

Riley then wrenched harder on the chain, trying to break it. Daniel felt the chain tightening on his neck and knocked Riley's hand away.

'Go to hell,' Daniel said defiantly, breaking free. There was a flash and Riley shot backwards, landing on the Slippery Geeks. He struck them so hard with his outstretched arms that they went sprawling into a group of pupils.

'Oy, watch out,' a girl called.

'Did you see that?' said another. 'He sent Riley flying.'

'Who is he?'

'I think he's Spooky Brady.'

Daniel didn't hang around. He ran, bumping into Miss Tubble, who was heading his way. 'Sorry – I didn't see you.'

'Out of my way, Daniel Brady!' She scowled, barging past him. He watched as she charged along the corridor, forcing Riley and the Geeks apart.

'What's going on?' asked Sophie. 'I heard that you hit Riley. What did you do?'

'Oh, nothing,' replied Daniel, smirking, holding up the chain with his thumb. 'We just sorted Riley out. I mean, the chain did – I think.'

Sophie sighed. 'I don't want any trouble; we'd better go. Riley's probably really angry.'

Riley's harsh voice echoed aggressively through the corridor. 'I'm gonna get you two!' He was fuming, and getting angrier by the minute. He searched for Daniel and Sophie, but they cleverly kept out of the way and when school ended Riley stomped home alone, his fists clenched.

Riley's home was a small terraced house in an impoverished neighbourhood, where kids wreak havoc and litter blows freely. He lived with his mum, stepdad and six-year-old brother.

That evening, Riley lay in bed, tossing and turning. He could hear the television blaring downstairs and his mum talking with his stepdad. Riley didn't like his stepdad because he used to flick his ears and made jokes about him.

Ten o'clock passed, then eleven. Eventually the noise faded into a quiet drone and Riley drifted off into a deep sleep – to dream about Daniel's chain.

It was dark and silent when a strange light penetrated Riley's eyelids.

'What's that?' he asked, staring at the mist drifting around the bed.

'I'm the Ghost of Children Past,' groaned a deep voice. Riley buried his head beneath the covers and gripped it tightly with both hands. He slowly lowered the bed covers, focusing on the shadowy walls. No one's there, he thought. He peered into the dark corners of the room, imagining faces. He noticed a strange ghost-like mist and panicked. His eyes grew wider as the mist swirled then formed into a tall ghost. Riley lay motionless. The ghost pointed and a light emerged from his finger, hitting Riley.

Where am I now? thought Riley. Children and noisy machinery spread out all around him. Boys and girls worked bent over metal bars that shifted in and out, clanging and banging, weaving back and forth. Huge wheels and pulleys towered above them, grinding, squeaking and turning. Riley clapped his hands over his ears. The noise is deafening, he thought – and it smells like the elephant house at the zoo.

Children of all ages were dressed in rags and hard at work. Some as young as five crawled under machines, while older ones carried baskets and others swept floors and cleaned. Everyone kept busy, except for Riley, looking at the silhouette of Daniel Brady, standing next to a ghost.

It looks like some kind of factory, thought Riley. Am I in a cotton mill?

'Yes, an eighteenth-century one,' came a voice.

Riley stared at Daniel and the ghost.

'Who are those skinny, scruffy-looking kids?' he asked. 'They're sad.' Suddenly a boy dropped a basket. 'Clumsy idiot,' laughed Riley. His eyes then flashed to a mean-looking man wearing a shabby dark suit and wielding a long stick. The man strolled sneakily towards the boy. He struck the boy's back with the stick.

'Ooh, I felt that,' said Riley, sniggering.

The skinny boy fell on his knees, sobbing.

'Now pick up the basket,' cursed the man. 'And all of you brats, get back to work – unless you want the same.'

Children scurried everywhere. A frail girl with clumps of hair missing stooped, grabbing a basket of cloth near Riley.

'What happened to your hair?' asked Riley. But she didn't reply. Riley became angry. 'Hey, I'm speaking to you.'

Still no answer came.

He tried to push the girl, but his hand went through

her. 'Help! You're not real,' he said. 'Clear off, you – you thing.' Riley flinched away, scared.

Confused, he headed along the factory floor. He trudged past the children, trying to touch them, flinching as his hand went straight through them. Then an old piece of paper floated in front of him, landing on the wooden floor. He picked it up and read the words on it:

*Birchton, Farmley Mills*
*Birchton, Dene*
*To the proprietor, Mr Farmley, dated this day 1833*

*We intervene in the misuse of child labour in factories and seek to advise the government. All will know the cruel practices carried out in your establishment and the atrocities that occur there.*

*You employ children as young as four years, known as scavengers, to crawl under machines. Children of all ages work for sixteen hours per day for a shilling a month. Children are severely beaten, and you are accountable for thirty deaths so far. The meals you provide would barely keep a dog alive, let alone a human being. Along with others, you are wicked and a curse to the Industrial Revolution. You will be punished for your actions.*

'I don't know what happened back then, and I don't care,' said Riley, feeling a shiver run down his spine. Suddenly, he heard a snarl, followed by an angry roar. Riley saw footprints in the dust. He turned to run, but a ghostly figure swept him off his feet, holding him up in the air by his collar.

'What's going on? Put me down!' demanded Riley. He wriggled and twisted until he saw who had hold of him. A terrifying monster ghost carried him off. He spun in and out of doorways, up and down large wooden staircases, along passages of the factory, seeing all the children working. Soon they drifted into a dingy room full of children who sat on rickety wooden benches on either side of long wooden tables. Riley stood still. 'Where am I?'

At one end of the room smaller boys and girls sat. All were barefoot. The ghost held Riley up to look at boys dressed in dirty shirts and knee-length trousers. The ghost swivelled Riley around to look at the girls, clothed in raggedy, filthy dresses. All the children had straggly, dirty hair.

At the other end of the room sat older boys and girls. Some wore shoes, but all were dirty and equally ragged. On the tables lay blackened bread and half-filled cans of a milky-looking substance. There were no plates, knives or forks, just the unappetising meal. All eyes focused on a tall spindly man with long hair.

'Older boys first!' he commanded. The first row of grubby, underfed boys rushed to queue at a small opening. One by one, they held out the tail ends of their shirts and in plopped a small portion of hot potatoes. They rushed back to devour their meagre meal of black bread, slop and potatoes, then licked their lips for more.

The next wave of children, the older girls, walked more gracefully to the serving hatch. They held up their greasy aprons to store their measly allowance. Then they scurried back to their respective places, where each quickly ate their ration.

It wasn't long before all of them looked anxiously about for more. The older ones ran to the tables of the younger children to grab every crumb and scrap that was left.

The children were bony, undernourished and helpless. The overseers constantly walked along the aisles, kicking the backs of children's legs.

Riley grimaced, then held his leg, cruelly imitating their reaction and pain. 'That must really hurt; I'm glad it's not me.'

The ghost became angry at Riley and whisked him up by his trousers, suspending him on a wooden beam.

'Help me!' Riley called out. But no one heard except one small blind boy. He pointed at Riley.

'I can hear him!' he said excitedly. 'I can! Look!'

The children all looked up, laughing. 'There's nothing up there.'

***

Darkness crept, silently, over the room.

'It's dark in here,' said Riley, stooping. He had straps tied over his shoulder. 'What's this on my back?'

A faint light revealed a narrow tunnel. Riley heard an eerie laugh from behind. He jerked his head around, then screamed. 'A skeleton!'

The skeleton rattled its bones. 'You have to pull this

101

cart full of coal, Riley. Find out what it would have been like to live like one of those poor children…'

Riley looked at the low ceiling and narrow sides of the passage, barely big enough for him to stand up in. Toxic gas filled his nostrils and the sound of trickling water splattered softly in the distance. He looked at the mini railway track then realised he had been placed in a coal mine.

'Go on, then! Pull as hard as you can,' demanded the skeleton, 'or else you'll stay here forever and end up like me.'

Riley bent and began to pull the heavy cart.

It wasn't long before the light faded and darkness fell.

'Keep pulling while I have a nap,' said the skeleton, chuckling. 'You laughed at the mill workers and so the Ghost of Children Past decided you should have a ride in a ghost mine, ha, ha, ha – with me.'

Beads of sweat trickled down Riley's face as he puffed, pulling the truck along the tracks. He licked his parched lips and struggled to walk. The heat began to take its toll.

'There is a light at the end of the tunnel,' claimed the skeleton. 'Pull harder.'

There was a creak, like a door opening.

'Who's there?' asked a voice.

Riley stopped. 'Riley. Riley's my name.'

'I'm the trapper. You must be the new boy.'

'Yes,' replied Riley nervously, straining to see the young boy. 'But I don't belong here.'

'Nor me. I sit 'ere on me own, in the dark, opening an' shuttin' the doors for the carts to go through – 'tis scary all on me' own.'

Riley wiped the sweat from his forehead. 'I'm trapped! How do I get out of here?'

Slowly, the skeleton sat upright and produced a faint glowing light that lit up the tunnel, revealing a number of enormous brown rats, moving creepily towards them. 'Riley,' he said. 'Your task is only to pull me – unless you want the trapper's job.' Riley looked at the trapper, who appeared to be about his similar age. His face and body were covered in coal smudges. The light began to fade. Riley decided to move forward in the tunnel. The trapper boy squinted when he saw the cart move away up the slope.

'Can you leave me some light?' the trapper boy called in hope.

Riley tugged the cart along in the dark, mumbling, 'Let me out of 'ere an' I promise to be good.'

Wearily, he pressed on, cursing the uneven ground beneath his feet. He pulled the cart faster. 'Is that a light up ahead?'

The light grew brighter. He approached a larger opening. Eventually he emerged from the tunnel.

Riley stared at a huge cave full of boys. Some had baskets of coal on their backs, struggling to walk, while others crouched over mechanical trays that carried coal past washers. Many boys picked debris from the coal. Their cramped positions looked unbearable. The boys all sat hunched forward. Looking closely at the boys' hands, he could see that all had sustained injuries from the machinery, such as crushed fingers, cuts and broken hands. Carts laden with coal lined the tracks and men poured the baskets of coal into troughs.

Riley ran eagerly towards the men. 'Help,' he pleaded. 'Hey, you lot, get me out of 'ere.'

But in the blink of an eyelid they vanished. He opened his eyes and found himself in a large, posh room filled with old antique furniture. Riley patted the dust off his clothes. 'Where on earth am I now?' he asked angrily.

'Right, let's be 'avin you,' said a wiry old man. 'Let's cover up this furniture.'

The surprised Riley asked, 'Who are you?'

The old man didn't answer. Instead he threw sheets over all the furniture, covering Riley in the process. Eventually Riley crawled out.

'Why did you do that, you old git?'

But the old man didn't reply. Riley then caught sight of a young skinny boy, covered in black dust, almost naked, standing in the fireplace, holding a piece of rag. The old man cupped his hands together for the boy to stand on.

'Up you go, lad, and be quick about it,' the old man grumbled. Riley watched the boy disappear up a chimney, followed by a flutter of dust falling. He backed cautiously away then hid behind a large chair. Riley had never seen such a grand room. It had life-size paintings and ornamental lights. He thought perhaps the queen lived there. His eyes were drawn to a suit of armour, a shield, and crossed swords. On the adjacent wall hung a life-size painting of a man in a black cloak.

Riley spotted something. He thought he saw the ghost walk across the floor, but then his attention was diverted by a noise. There was a soft thud from the chimney. A heap of black soot hit the cloth on the hearth. A groaning sob followed.

'Stop complaining about yer sores,' snarled the man, looking up the chimney, holding a rod in his hand. 'Get up higher,' he demanded. 'Or I'll take the needle stick to yer feet.'

'You animal – leave him alone!' protested Riley.

'Who said that?' growled the man, looking around the room.

'I did,' blurted the brave, but nervous, invisible Riley.

'Where are yer, then? Show me, so I can brain yer.'

Riley stood up from behind the chair to face the man, but he couldn't see Riley so he called out again. 'Come on, where are yer?'

More soot dropped from the chimney and splattered on the man. He frantically tried to brush it off, cursing and threatening the boy up the chimney. Suddenly, there was a loud tearing noise. Riley's eyes flashed to the life-size painting of the cloaked man. The cloaked man's eyes peered to one side. He glared into the room. Then his body began to swell and he stepped from the painting, a deformed coal monster with devilish eyes.

He headed towards the old man, who cowered away, whimpering.

'I want revenge for all the dead chimney boys.' The coal monster pounded across the floor, his fists clenched like rocks and eyes red with anger. He thundered towards the fireplace.

Riley jumped out of his way, but tripped, hitting the floor with a thump. Dazed and confused, he looked at the ceiling then at the window.

'What on earth was that noise, and why are you on the floor?' asked his mum.

Riley looked all around, confused. 'I-I-I just had a nightmare, Mum. I must have fallen out of bed.'

# Chapter 14

The Geeks stood in the west wing corridor of the school, listening to Riley tell them about his nightmare.

'It was nasty. I dreamed of these scruffy-looking kids being tortured. And there were monsters and ghosts, and a coal mine with dirty kids. You two wouldn't have liked them. I was never really scared, though. That reminds me – Brady threw us somehow. Let's go look for him.'

In the meantime, Daniel had his eyes fixed on another plaque on the wall.

'I saw some writing like this in my books. I think this plaque may come from the castle. It has really inspiring words. I love it, and – it may give us a clue.' Daniel read the words on the plaque out loud:

*Go to battle with courage.*
*Your quest awaits you each day*
*The strength that has carried you this far*
*Can take you the rest of the way.*

Sophie kept a watchful eye out. 'Yes, Daniel, I like the words too – only Riley's around here somewhere,' she said apprehensively. 'He always turns up.'

Tyler looked behind. 'Oh no, speak of the devil.'

'There they are! Get them!'

Sophie and Tyler turned and ran. Daniel clutched his chain, but it was too late; Riley and the Geeks landed abruptly at Daniel's side and began to strut around him, puffing and panting.

'Got you now, Brady, 'aven't we?' Riley said, coughing. Daniel held on to his chain as the three sauntered menacingly around him. Riley's eyes lingered on Daniel's chain. 'How did you do it?' he asked.

Daniel edged away. 'Do what?'

Riley leaned closer to Daniel and whispered in his ear. 'How did you throw me? It was like magic. An' I had a weird dream last night – like it was real. Do you know anything about that?'

Daniel waved his hand to repel Riley's bad breath. 'Perhaps someone is trying to tell you something.'

Riley chuckled. 'Like what? That you're a spook? Come on, Brady, what's going on?'

Daniel wasn't having it. 'Nothing is going on, so clear off.'

Sophie and Tyler watched from a distance as Riley and Daniel argued.

'Getting brave again, are we?' mocked Riley, standing with his arms around the Geeks' shoulders. 'What d'ya think we should do with him, lads?'

The Geeks didn't reply. They just smirked, so Riley pushed them forward to frighten Daniel. 'Give Brady a little dig,' he said. So the Geeks took it in turn to sneakily prod Daniel.

'He feels like jelly,' one Geek joked.

'More like skin and bone,' said the other. Just then, a flash of light sparked from each of the Geeks' hands. They jumped out of their skin, shrieking and waving their hands in the air. Horrified, they looked at their fingers: the skin was melting away to bone.

Riley winced. 'You're turning into skeletons! Look at your fingers!' Frantically, the Geeks ran in circles, looking at their hands in horror. Riley stood with his mouth open as boys and girls laughed at them ... until Daniel grabbed the Geeks' hands.

'Are you two nuts?' he asked. 'There's nothing wrong with your fingers.'

But the Geeks weren't convinced, and neither was Riley. They leaped away from Daniel.

'I knew it – you did something,' Riley claimed. 'Didn't you?' He and the Geeks nodded briefly at each other then turned and ran. They sprinted so fast along the corridor that they swished all the leaflets off the wall, before disappearing around the corner.

Sophie was the first to rush back to Daniel. 'What did you do?'

Daniel held up his fist. 'Magic – I got them again.'

Tyler arrived, glancing behind him. 'We were with you.'

'I know, Tyler – I noticed you hiding behind Sophie for protection.'

The next lesson saw Daniel bury his head in a book, studying – but it wasn't science. He was reciting some of the words he had read on the plaques:

*Your quest awaits you each day.*
*If there is darkness, I will provide you with comfort and light.*
*Your powerful dreams will inspire you.*

He thought, I remember dreaming about the school in darkness. I could see the crossover link and I sensed danger in the air. Daniel puzzled over the words for an hour, concluding that the path across the courtyard in the winter never had lights on outside. It was pitch black and forever in darkness. Was this a clue? The crossover link between the four points: the north, south, east and west corridors? He was eager to explore more at break.

After class, he beckoned Sophie and Tyler to follow him. 'We've got to look at something,' Daniel said.

They arrived at the courtyard link and looked out of the window at the small sections of gardens. Daniel studied his notes. 'Now, let me think … we're in the middle, but there's nothing here. We've got to look outside.'

'You can go first,' Tyler said.

Sophie reminded them, 'It's out of bounds.' But Daniel didn't hesitate. He opened the door and stepped out onto the pathway, shadowed by Sophie, with Tyler bringing up the rear. They strolled out onto the grass and Daniel spotted something over near the wall of the east wing.

Riley and the Geeks had followed them, and watched

them from a window. Riley didn't take his eyes off Daniel. He wanted to know his every move.

'Why is Brady in the garden?' he asked. 'Keep your eyes on them.'

Daniel had spotted a carving on the wall hidden below a stone figure. 'Look!' he said excitedly. 'It's a carving of clasped hands, like my chain – and look! There's a scary face, just like in my dream.' Tyler's and Sophie's eyes flashed to and fro. They looked at each other, then at Daniel, then at his chain, baffled by the resemblance.

'This is too scary,' Sophie said, looking around.

'Yeah, man, let's get out of here.'

'Don't be wimps,' Daniel said. 'Let's see if there's anything else.' He ran his hand over the rough stone carving and it began to make a grating sound. The ground beneath their feet moved and the wall shook. Daniel slid forward. Desperately, he grabbed hold of Sophie and Tyler – but, as he did so, all three fell through the shiny opening and were swallowed up. They disappeared as the wall closed behind them.

'Did yer see that?' asked Riley. 'They just vanished! Where did they go? Quick – follow me.' Riley and the Geeks ran along the corridor and out into the garden, then approached the wall with caution. Riley pushed the Geeks closer to the wall carvings. 'Move forward, you two,' he ordered. 'Now, run your hands over that face.'

'You do it,' one Geek replied.

Riley barged the Geeks aside. 'Outta my way, then,' he snapped, pushing the carving, the wall, and all around it. Nothing happened. His face turned red with anger.

'What's going on out there?' barked Miss Griffin, craning her head through an open window. 'You three are out of bounds.'

Daniel, Sophie and Tyler stood, in darkness, on muddy grass, looking at the front of a castle that stretched out in front of them. It looked like a fortress. It had dimly lit windows and several turrets. A bright moon revealed other buildings to each side, and a line of trees surrounded the grounds. Daniel could see, behind the castle, the outline of houses, chimneys and metal railings. The air was fresh and cool, and the hoot of an owl broke the eerie silence.

'This is really spooky,' Sophie whispered, starting to cry.

Nervously, Tyler said, 'Get us back. How did we get here?'

Daniel was scared too. 'This place looks like the old castle and manor. I've seen sketches of them.'

They heard dogs barking in the distance, and the moon disappeared behind a cloud.

Sophie peeked over her shoulder. 'We've had it.'

'How did this happen, Daniel?'

'Don't know,' said Daniel, looking towards the old castle and the manor. 'We'd better get away from here.'

The three huddled together and crept along the winding path towards the manor until they came to a window.

Sophie stretched up, peering in. 'I can't see anybody.'

Tyler rubbed his sleeve on the glass. 'No one there.

Shouldn't we go back?'

'Look out,' shouted Daniel. They all ducked as a ghostly figure suddenly flew out of the window. 'What on earth? *Look!* There it goes!' They sat staring at the strange image as it flew over the trees and chimney pots before disappearing into the night.

Sophie turned to Daniel. 'We've got to get out of here.'

Tyler leaned closer. 'Don't worry, we will.' He swivelled around to Daniel. *'Won't we?'*

'Good idea, Tyler,' Daniel said, pushing him towards a door. 'Lead the way.'

'No, no, please,' begged Tyler.

'Shush – listen,' whispered Daniel. 'I can hear voices. Someone's coming. Quick, let's hide.'

They crept behind a small outbuilding and waited, holding their breath. Daniel whispered, 'There's a man and a woman, carrying lamps.'

They watched in silence. The man lifted the large door knocker. *Clang – clang.* A hinge creaked loudly then a ray of light shone out from the house, as bright as a hundred searchlights. The wind howled as it sucked the man and woman into the building, then the door slammed shut.

'I'm not going in there,' whispered Sophie.

'Me neither, no way, man.' Daniel had already begun walking over to the same door. He looked back, to see Tyler and Sophie still hiding.

'This place is too scary,' said Sophie. 'Let's go.'

'Go where?' asked Tyler, rolling his eyes.

Daniel beckoned them over. 'Come on, you two. Buddy Wizard's in here – you'll see.' They reluctantly tiptoed to Daniel.

Tyler looked up to the moon. 'It's scary with that shining on us, casting shadows everywhere.'

'That's just the moon, you idiot,' said Daniel. 'I'm scared too, but you and Sophie shouldn't be petrified.' At that moment, the door creaked loudly again.

Daniel turned to face the door. 'Quick! Come on, it's letting us in. I've got my chain to protect us.'

Sophie and Tyler waited, undecided, until the howling of dogs broke the silence.

'Okay, okay, I'm coming,' Tyler said, rushing to Daniel's side.

Reluctantly, Sophie stepped closer. 'I don't like this, Daniel.' One by one they went through the doorway. The door slammed shut behind them. They stood in a dirty, poorly lit entrance hall with cold grey walls. The floor was wooden and sloped, making it difficult to walk straight. The clonk of their shoes echoed through the walls as they desperately tried to be quiet.

'Look, Daniel,' gasped Sophie, peering at a plaque on the wall. 'That is like – but it can't be – surely it's not the one in our school?'

They crept nervously up to the plaque.

'No way, bro.'

'Yeah. Scary, but cool.' Daniel read one encouraging bit. 'Your powerful dreams will inspire your noble action.'

Two ugly charcoal portraits hung on the cracked

walls, and cobwebs trailed menacingly from them, their thick strands indicating the presence of some enormous spiders. Daniel picked up an old book that lay on a table and brushed away the dust. He opened the cover and jumped. The remains of a flattened spider stared up at him. He promptly flicked the pages over and dislodged the grisly remains onto Tyler's shoe.

Daniel carefully turned the pages of the book. 'There are lots of names in here. Listen.

*Log book Middleton Manor 1856*
*21 August*
*Fever has spread again. One more death – Jud Oxley.*
*10 September*
*Mr Ferris had reason to strap pupil John Hunt. Bleeding stopped, but red marks needed ointment.*
*6 October*
*Two deaths occurred from fever.*
*14 November*
*Sent for Mrs Jackson, Moat Lane. Her daughter's hair is overrun with vermin.*
*15 December*
*Weather extremely cold. All children are poorly clad, and barefoot. Will endeavour to raise temperature from stove.*
*18 December*
*Had need to strap Foggerty again. Severe cold. Many children have frostbite.*
*20 December*
*More are falling ill.'*

The three stood silent as Daniel slowly closed the book.

'Nasty,' stated Daniel. 'Everyone should know what happened in the past, including Bullfrog Riley.'

'Yes definitely,' agreed Sophie. 'That sounds awful.'

'Me too, yeah.'

Look, there's another door here,' said Sophie, pushing it open. She then held back, waiting for Daniel to lead the way. They cautiously entered a room that smelled musty and was poorly lit by three gas lamps perched on window sills. Rows of benches faced an old table.

'This looks like a dingy old classroom,' Daniel remarked. 'The plaque... Wow! Look! It's the one in our school. I told you!'

They gazed in awe.

'See – it does read the same: *fear not the task*. I knew it!'

Sophie and Tyler nodded in agreement, still in shock, until Daniel tried to pick up the plaque. It crumbled into dust and vanished.

Sophie and Tyler held their breath, speechless.

Daniel gulped and brushed his hands. 'It's okay, I know where it is. Look – there's a stove and a picture on the wall. It looks like a queen.'

However, Sophie was staring elsewhere, nudging Daniel to look.

'Uh-oh,' he said. 'That looks like a ghost.'

Tyler began to take giant steps to the left. 'Let's go, man.'

'Wait,' Daniel suggested. 'Don't move – it may be

friendly.'

Sophie edged away with Tyler. 'It doesn't look friendly.'

Suddenly the ghost disappeared.

'Oh no,' said Tyler. 'Look!'

Boys and girls began to appear everywhere. Seats began to fill up with dirty-looking, barefoot children wearing stained, raggedy clothes. The children were all awfully thin, with matted hair. Just then, a tall, stocky teacher wearing a flowing black jacket and carrying a long stick strolled menacingly into the class, the children fell silent. He had a drawn face and dark streaked hair that hung over his mean-looking eyes. He paced slowly up and down in front of his desk.

Sophie tapped Daniel on the shoulder and whispered, 'Can he see us?'

'I don't think so,' replied Daniel, shivering.

*Crack!* The long stick hit the table and everyone in the room jumped along with Sophie. The teacher glared all around. 'Be seated, you ugly rascals.'

'Oh no, he's spotted us,' said Sophie, moving to sit down.

Daniel grabbed her hand. 'Wait – sit down slowly.'

Sophie bowed her head then whispered, 'Are you sure he can't see us?'

Tyler stood, rigid. 'I hope not.'

The boys and girls sat with small pieces of slate and chalk, copying the words that the teacher wrote on the blackboard. Lots of children made mistakes, and the teacher became angry. He frowned and scowled until he finally blew his top, dragging a boy off the bench by his hair. *Whack! Whack!* He hit the boy on the head.

'I'll teach you a lesson you won't forget!'

Tyler looked at Daniel. 'What if he comes near us?'

The teacher glared around the room then struck another boy nearby.

'Let's go,' said Daniel, holding on to his chain. 'We're not staying here.'

The nasty teacher dragged a girl by her hair along the aisle, swinging his cane, striking several others as he went.

'Leave her alone,' pleaded Tyler.

Sophie angrily gripped the bench they sat on. 'Stop it, you bully!'

Suddenly, the bench began to rock. Sophie screamed. The teacher let go of the girl. Slowly, he ambled towards Daniel, Tyler and Sophie.

Tyler wiped his forehead. 'He's coming this way.'

Sophie looked ill.

Daniel got up, a bit wobbly, and opened his eyes.

'Everyone has gone,' he said. 'Look over there! I think it's another ghost.' They ducked as a ghostly figure flew towards them and drifted through a door at the end of the room.

'Let's get out of here,' said Daniel. 'We need to follow that.'

'No,' answered Tyler swiftly.

'Nor me,' replied Sophie.

'We've got to,' said Daniel. 'We can't stay here.'

Reluctantly, Sophie and Tyler agreed. They crept

through the door into a dimly lit passage. An old man carrying a gas lamp walked ahead of them. Daniel stopped, pointing to the wall. 'It's the other plaque – the same as the school one. It's here hanging up – and the first line reads the same. *Study to learn.*'

'Don't touch it,' gasped Tyler.

'I won't.'

'This is freaky. If my mum only knew…'

A row of glowing candles hung from the walls.

'They look a bit like the school lights – there may be old dungeons that way.'

Tyler quickly turned. 'I take it we go the other way, then?'

Daniel gripped his chain. 'Hang on – I've got an idea.'

'No, not again, please.' said Sophie. 'Look what happened last t-t-time.'

All three saw the old man flash past them. They went through rooms where children huddled together on straw beds, then along stairways and passages, twisting and turning until they stopped in front of three scary-looking ghosts.

'Where are we, Daniel?' asked Tyler. 'It's dark.'

'I only held my chain; we didn't move.'

Sophie didn't budge; she stared ahead as one ghost circled them, gradually changing into a familiar shape.

'Buddy Wizard,' said Daniel.

'Yes, Daniel, that's what you call me. Though now is not the time. The others are not pleased. They are angry ghosts and I am trying to appease them.'

'It's my fault,' Daniel said. 'I wanted to find out more.'

Tyler and Sophie had their eyes closed. They couldn't move.

'For centuries there have been young and old bullies. On their deaths, many of their victims cried out for revenge and cursed their tormentors. Many spirits arose, and were named Punishers. I am one of those. I, like many, was a young orphan. Any magic I possess was given to me by an ancestor who was a magician. You awoke my spirit when you climbed the tree at your school. I could sense your presence through the branches of the tree; the fear you had was the fear I could feel. I sent the message on the tree. I made the plaque. My spirit was touched – so you unlocked me. For hundreds of years, our tortured souls yearned for revenge. Now, we have risen once again. Some are now witches or warlocks. Others seek to do kind deeds. You must leave this place, Daniel. You must go now – without delay.'

In a puff of ghostly mist they found themselves standing in front of a stone face embedded in a wall. On either side of the face was a carving of a hand clasping a dagger.

Buddy Wizard held up his hand. The wall shone and a light shot towards Daniel's chain. The glow rebounded to Sophie then Tyler – and they disappeared.

# Chapter 15

In the meantime, Riley and the Geeks edged away from the wall, puzzled about where Daniel, Sophie and Tyler had gone. They walked through the garden, back into the school, Riley deep in thought. 'I can't understand what happened out there. What do you two think?'

They just shrugged.

Miss Griffin had spotted them. 'What are you three doing out there?' she asked.

'Brady set us up, Miss,' replied Riley. 'He was out there, with his friends, and they just disappeared. We only went to look for him. He forced us to go out of bounds. He's spooky.'

'I've heard you've been picking on Daniel Brady, so stop it. I don't think you lot are that innocent either, so don't hang around here – off you go.'

Riley and the Geeks kept looking out of the window as they pretended to saunter casually away.

'All right, let's go back. She's gone.'

They didn't stop looking out of the window for Daniel. Just then, Riley's eyes lit up. Daniel, Tyler and Sophie reappeared in the garden. But the persistent Miss Griffin had followed Riley to the window.

'Look! There they are!' Riley said, laughing.

'Good try, Billy Riley,' barked Miss Griffin, pouncing and peering down at him. 'I suppose they've just appeared out of thin air? Don't be daft. You're all on report – follow me.'

'But Miss, wait, look,' complained Riley.

'Now!' she demanded, striding away, the Geeks immediately following.

Riley trudged behind, looking back. 'I know I saw Brady. I'll get him.'

Daniel, Sophie and Tyler crept out of the garden into the school's crossover link. 'Thank God we're back,' Daniel said. 'I can't understand what happened.' He twiddled with his chain. 'One minute we were here – the next minute there – and now we're back again.'

Sophie and Tyler seemed to be in a trance. They just briefly stared back at him.

'I know what you're both thinking,' Daniel continued. 'We're not going out there again – just in case.'


Billy Riley wanted others to poke fun at Daniel, Sophie and Tyler so he spread rumours about them seeing ghosts. The next few days at school were difficult for Daniel, Tyler and Sophie. They had spoken about the school being haunted and that was enough for Riley and the other kids to tease them about ghosts and spooks.

'We are going to put a stop to this sort of behaviour,' said Mr Shaw, speaking to Miss White. 'We keep hearing about bullying – and blow me if I didn't have a strange dream about bullying as well.' Mr Shaw peered over the top of his glasses, and spotted Daniel walk past. 'Ah,

Daniel, just the person,' he said. 'Has anything strange happened to you lately? Children are talking about you.'

Daniel went hot, then cold. 'No, sir.' He then looked straight into Miss White's probing eyes and blushed. '*Honest,* Miss.'

'What about your friends, Sophie Little and Tyler Topping?' she asked. 'Has anything strange happened to them? Some children are talking about them too.'

Daniel gazed at the ground. 'No, Miss. Can I go now?'

'Yes, okay. Your friends seem to be waiting for you.'

Sophie didn't waste any time. She ran to greet Daniel. 'They're on to us,' she said, looking worried.

'What do you mean?'

'We've been asked lots of questions about you, Daniel.'

'Who's asked about me?'

Tyler intervened. 'The headmaster has. Sophie just came out with it about Buddy Wizard. She didn't mean to. I think you can guess the rest.'

'But you know he's real now, don't you?'

Tyler and Sophie nodded, while Daniel paced the floor.

'You are convinced, aren't you?'

'No, I think I should tell my parents.'

'Me too,' answered Tyler.

Later that day, the three strolled out of the school.

'There they are,' said one girl. 'The three nerds.'

'Brady's scary,' taunted another.

Daniel, Sophie and Tyler walked quickly on, ignoring

them.

'Had a good day at school, Daniel?' asked Mrs Brady, arranging her flowers, when Daniel got home.

'Sort of, Mum – you wouldn't believe what happened.'

'My plant has grown some new buds. What do you want to tell me?'

'OK. I'll try to explain.' Daniel told his mum some of the happenings, until Emily came in. She overheard their conversation and butted in. 'He's in a daydream, Mum. He imagines everything.'

'Well, it does seem strange.'

Daniel retorted, 'I don't imagine everything. The ghost is real. So get lost, Emily.'

Emily pushed past Daniel. 'You're a nightmare.'

Their mum ignored the argument and continued talking to her plants.

Daniel shot out of the room, slamming the door behind him.

'You're just a spoilt brat, Emily,' he yelled, running up the stairs.

That evening, by choice, Daniel went to bed early. He lay in bed, wiping away his tears and cuddling up to Chip. 'They keep picking on me, Chip. I've had enough of them – and that school.'

Chip wagged his tail then licked Daniel's hand.

'I suppose I'll wake up feeling better, Chip. I always do.' Daniel had begun to drift off to sleep, but then his bedroom door opened.

'What's this letter all about?' asked his dad. Daniel

opened his eyes.

'The headmaster says you're frightening the kids at school, something about ghosts and magic? You haven't got any future if you keep imagining things – not in cars, anyway.'

'I'm not imagining things, Dad. They're lying. All these odd things are happening to me. I've been having strange dreams.' But his dad left the room, not listening to him. Daniel pulled the covers over his head. He sat up and beckoned Chip out of hiding. 'Listen, Chip,' he whispered. 'I can hear them talking about me. I'm always causing trouble. I'm going to run away.'

Daniel sobbed himself to sleep – and dreamed of Buddy Wizard.

Daniel gazed at the eerie mist swirling around the bedroom. He got out of bed, peering through the mist, and imagined a ghostly figure beckoning him to follow. Daniel tiptoed silently along the landing, past the bedroom doors and down the stairs, Chip following closely. The front door opened then closed with a soft click. Daniel felt something nudge the back of his legs. Turning nervously, he came face to face with the front of his dad's vintage car – being driven by Buddy Wizard. The boy ghost opened the driver's door, beckoning Daniel to sit in the car.

'Okay,' said Daniel, walking forward. 'This is an odd dream, but I'll go with it.'

'You will be the driver. Here, take these.' Buddy Wizard handed Daniel a pair of goggles and a thick white coat.

'How am I going to drive?' asked Daniel, placing Chip on the seat beside him. Suddenly, the car started, the headlights came on, and the gear lever moved. The car chugged along the driveway then onto the road. Daniel grabbed the steering wheel, veered to the left and then to the right, and began following the cat's eyes in the road. As his confidence grew, he swerved around corners, the tyres screeching. Soon he was changing gear confidently and speeding. He drove fast through the empty suburban streets while Buddy Wizard slept.

'Look at me, Chip – who says I won't be into cars?'

Chip barked softly in agreement.

Daniel arrived at the city centre and slowed down. He gave way at roundabouts, beckoned to mystified drivers, and waved at the odd pedestrian. He steered over bridges, through tunnels, and alongside a train, where a few passengers pointed at him.

Daniel became braver. 'Let's see what it can do, Chip.' Faster and faster he drove along the deserted road, looking sideways at the speeding train, not noticing the bend in the road, or how close he was to the train, until he saw a barrier across the road. The train hooted. Daniel panicked. The car flew over the barrier, heading towards the train. There was a whoosh and a thud as the wheels clipped the top of the barrier. The car tilted sideways and veered off alongside the train. Frightened faces looked out. Daniel grimaced then steered the car downward, away from the train. He managed to turn the wheel to the left and the car went left. He pushed the steering wheel forward, and the car went down. He pulled the steering wheel back, and the car headed up.

'This is easier, Chip, I've got the hang of it.'

Chip barked as if to agree. But Daniel had more serious thoughts. *I had better take the car back now.*

He leaned over the side of the car above the street lamps of Old Furrow Way, twenty metres above the ground, then ten metres, then two metres. Confidently, Daniel swung the car into the drive a metre from the ground – but unfortunately he hit the squirrel sign with a bang. The headlights went out and the car dropped to the ground with an almighty crash, flattening the wheels. All four doors fell off.

'Well, that will have woken everyone around,' said Buddy Wizard.

Daniel ran around the wrecked car. 'Oh no! Please hide me, Buddy.'

The front door opened. Out came Mr Brady with a torch. 'What on earth?' he groaned, staring at the remains of his vintage car. 'What the hell? My car! What's happened?' He watched for movement from his neighbours' houses. All remained quiet. No one stirred. Angrily, he turned and ran back to his front door to the waiting Mrs Brady, pushing her to one side as she attempted to peer outside. He grabbed his phone. 'Police, please.'

In the meantime, Daniel and Chip dodged past Mrs Brady and dashed upstairs – but ran headlong into Emily, who was walking down.

She screamed, falling back on the stairs, bumping on

her bottom down the last few steps.

'That's for picking on me,' Daniel said, peering at her from the top of the stairs.

Emily sat facing the front door. 'Daniel's torn all my clothes, Mum. They're in shreds on my bedroom floor!'

'What! No, surely not. Listen – I can hear something.' Mrs Brady plucked up her courage then ventured into the kitchen. Her eyes nearly popped out of their sockets at the sight that greeted her. 'My flowers,' she sobbed. 'My poor little things – their heads have gone. That's impossible.'

Emily turned around. 'I can hear a crunching noise coming from the conservatory.'

'Hold it! I'll go,' snarled the angry Mr Brady, picking up his cricket bat.

'We'll all go,' said Mrs Brady, following him. They tiptoed past the beheaded flowers and opened the conservatory door. Tall plants, thin plants and great big leafy plants leaned, lopsided, against each other.

Mrs Brady nearly fainted in shock. 'I don't want to look any more.'

Emily had a look through the door, pointing. 'It's there!'

Mr Brady lowered his cricket bat. 'It's some sort of animal. I thought it could be a burglar.'

'I can see it!' shrieked Mrs Brady. 'A green monster thing! Shoo! Shoo.'

'You must have frightened it, my dear,' suggested Mr Brady, wiping his forehead, 'when you looked at it.'

Daniel had a quick peep and hid behind them,

laughing.

The little monster was gnawing at a plant, glaring at Mrs Brady. Suddenly, it scampered up the glass and slithered head-first out of the window into the garden.

Emily poked at the plants with the broom. 'Ghosts, little monsters – where's Daniel?'

She raced past Daniel as if he wasn't there, ran upstairs and opened his bedroom door.

Daniel awoke with a start to the sun streaming through his bedroom window. Instantly he remembered the events of the previous night. Frantically he sat up. He knew he had heard someone at his bedroom door.

'Phew, I thought I was downstairs.' He yawned and stretched. 'Chip, where are you? I had such a weird dream.'

The little dog jumped on his bed, his ears pricked.

'I hope it *was* a dream. I hope it didn't really happen – but it felt so real…' Daniel jumped out of bed, knocked poor Chip flying, 'Sorry, Chip. I've got to check downstairs.'

Daniel crept silently down the stairs and along the hall – where he bumped straight into his mum, coming out of the lounge.

# Chapter 16

'I'm sure I heard noises here last night,' Mrs Brady said, looking around. 'And I had a horrible dream. I dreamed all my flowers had been eaten by a little green monster.'

'Well, that's not as bad as my nightmare,' said Mr Brady, walking down the stairs. 'I dreamed my car was in pieces on the driveway.'

Daniel opened the kitchen door in trepidation. 'Phew. The flowers are still there, Chip.' He wandered into the conservatory. 'It all looks the same to me, but wait…' Daniel ran through the hall, opened the front door and stared outside. 'The car's gone!'

'What are you playing at, Daniel?' asked his mum.

Daniel ran back to the kitchen then into the garden and surveyed everything through the garage window. 'I don't believe it! Dad's car is in the garage – and in one piece. That means Emily's clothes are all right too – damn.'

It was still early. Daniel had some time before he went to school. He dozed off at the kitchen table, a big smile on his face – even though Emily's clothes were still intact.

Daniel rode his bike to school that day, pedalling fast. He whizzed through fallen leaves along Old Furrow

Way, dodged around conkers and did a wheelie before cycling out onto the main road. It wasn't long before he arrived at school and locked his bike up in the bike shed. Daniel wanted to keep it a secret from Riley for as long as possible.

At break, Daniel told Sophie and Tyler about his dream last night.

Sophie kept quiet, her eyes fixed on Daniel's chain. 'Weird dreams, bullies, nasty men. What next?'

'I'm in trouble, though,' sighed Daniel. 'Mr Shaw and Miss White want to see me.'

'Come in here, Daniel.' Mr Shaw beckoned to him, peering over the top of his glasses. 'We just want a word with you about the rumours going around the school – about you seeing ghosts. They also involve your friends, Sophie Little and Tyler Topping. The headmaster is now involved. Don't worry, Daniel. We've heard some odd rumours about the school too. We can't discuss that now, but if you see anything, please tell us first, otherwise others may make fun of you, or you could frighten the newcomers.'

Miss White smiled. 'Sit down, Daniel. Unfortunately, we cannot change our Christmas play, which has ghosts in, so we thought you and your two friends could play the ghost parts. Then the children will think that's the reason you three have been talking about ghosts.'

Mr Shaw intervened. 'We would like this bullying and all the ghost stuff to stop. We don't want to sweep it under the carpet.'

Daniel suddenly thought of Miss Griffin's broomstick.

The carpet under his feet rippled. He quickly shifted sideways, trying to ignore it.

'Stop fidgeting – what's the matter?' Miss White asked. 'We know some pupils are picking on you, and thought it might be good for your confidence to have a part in the play. We have parts in the play for Sophie and Tyler too.'

Mr Shaw spoke again. 'We're putting notices up all over the school about this year's play and the names of the pupils taking part. Everyone will be jealous of you. How does that sound?'

'Wicked – but none of us have acted before. Will we be able to do it?'

Mr Shaw winked. 'I don't think you'll have any problem acting, Daniel, do you? Especially the parts we have in mind.'

Soon everybody knew who was going to be in the school play. Daniel, Sophie and Tyler studied the names on the noticeboard and the title of the play.

*Middleton High presents this year's Christmas Play:*
*The Ghosts of Middleton Manor*

Daniel pointed to their names. 'Riley isn't going to like this.'

That afternoon Daniel played football in PE. When they returned to the changing room, Tyler patted Daniel on the back. 'You had a good game.'

'So did you,' replied Daniel, fumbling in his kit bag then rummaging through his clothes. 'Where did I leave my chain?' He swept his hand along the bench. 'It's gone – my chain's gone. Has anyone seen it?'

Most of the boys shook their head or said no. One boy looked at Daniel's neck, sniggering then apologised. 'Sorry, Daniel, I haven't seen it. I just heard kids talking about it.'

'You can't have lost it,' said Tyler. 'You must have left it at home.'

'No, I took it off here – I think.'

They hunted everywhere, and kept looking until everyone had left the changing room. Daniel headed out of school and told Sophie. 'I lost my chain in PE. I'm sure I had it before the game.'

'Don't worry,' she replied. 'It'll turn up.'

That evening, Riley lay in bed, dangling Daniel's chain in the air. 'That'll teach Brady to try and make a fool of me,' he said, smirking. 'This will go nicely in my collection.'

Ten o'clock passed, then eleven o'clock. Riley fell fast asleep. All was quiet and peaceful in his bedroom. Riley began to dream … about ghosts.

'Billy Riley,' came a deep, mournful voice in his dream. 'Sad Billy Riley, foolish Billy Riley.'

'Who's there?' Riley asked, looking around his bedroom. He stared into the darkness and spotted the faint image of a face that rose up from the foot of his bed. *Am I seeing things?* His eyes fixed on the shadowy face that floated up, growing a body with arms and legs. The image began to grow taller. It moved forward still growing. A ghostly figure with piercing black eyes stepped out of the shadows and stood before him, wrapped in chains. The figure glared down at him.

'Billy Riley,' sneered the ghost. 'You are not the keeper of the chain, so I have come to warn you.'

There was a clang of metal and a long, shining chain dragged across the floor. Riley stared at a line of glowing hands that slithered, like a snake, up and onto his bed. He froze, mesmerised, feeling the chain of shiny hands climb up his body. The chain slid over his shoulders and wrapped around his chest.

The ghost stared at Riley, laughing. 'You're really hooked on me now, aren't you, Billy Riley?'

'No-n-no,' Riley said, shivering. 'L-let me go.'

The ghost stooped closer to Riley. 'I am the Ghost of Children's Judgement – and you're the accused.'

The ghost hauled Riley up by the chain and dangled him in the air.

'No, no, please let me go,' pleaded Riley.

'Remember the Ghost of Children Past?' asked the angry voice. 'Did you not learn *anything?*'

A strong wind blew, the window opened, and the ghost flew through, with Riley trailing behind. They disappeared.

'Where are we?' asked Riley, standing in bare feet on a cold stone floor, still wrapped in the chains. But no one answered. He looked warily around. He was in a long, dingy room with lots of decrepit metal cubicles. In each cubicle sat a small bathtub filled with motionless horrid brown water. Riley pinched his nose. 'Yuk, what a smell,' he said. 'Get me out of here.'

Suddenly, Riley heard voices from a distant doorway. Children began to appear. They were dirty, bedraggled and wore clothes that resembled sacks. He wanted somewhere to hide, but it was too late. Two policemen dressed in old-fashioned uniforms swaggered into the room. 'Will that be all of 'em?' asked one policeman in a gruff voice.

'Yep,' came the reply. 'The poor old horse can't tug any more than twenty. We've got ten thieves, six troublemakers, two real bad 'uns and two insane.'

The policeman pushed the boys and girls forward, past the bewildered Riley, towards the cubicles. Riley closed his eyes tightly. They approached him, but strode past without speaking. Carefully, Riley opened his eyes, wondering why the policemen didn't take any notice of him. He stood rooted to the spot, terrified, listening to the gentle swish of splashing water.

'They're not going to wash in that filthy water, are they?' Riley asked in horror.

One policeman replied. 'Who said the water's filthy?'

Riley closed his eyes, cringing. The policeman strolled around, tipped back his funny-looking helmet then scratched his head. Riley opened his eyes again and sighed with relief as the policeman walked away.

The splashing water stopped and the children fumbled for their grubby clothes. They hurriedly dressed, then scurried out to stand at the end of the room.

'Over there, you lot,' said one policeman. 'You're all gettin' a thorough search and all distinguishing marks noted down for our records.' He laughed. 'So let's be 'avin' yer.'

Riley edged to the opposite end of the room, looking for a way out. At that moment a scuffle broke out. A skinny boy tried to escape and ran towards the door. Riley dodged out of his way, but fell into the path of the pursuing policeman. Riley apologised.

'You better be sorry, lad,' growled the policeman, dragging the skinny boy by his ear past the invisible Riley. 'Now get back in line.'

Riley flinched as the boy ran through him. 'Argh! I'm invisible. Help! Mr Ghost, get me out of 'ere.' All heads turned towards Riley, but only one voice spoke.

A woman jailer pointed up in the air. 'Screams – you always 'ear screams. Kids usually shout in the night, though.'

A policeman laughed. 'Tomorrow is judgement day – that's when they'll scream.'

Riley was unable to move. The words *judgement day* echoed in his mind, again and again, until he was whisked away by the ghost once more.

Riley found himself sitting on a chair in the middle of a room, wrapped in his chains. He felt the chains move, pulsating as if the metal was alive. He looked nervously around him. Pupils from his school sat in rows behind him. Everything in the room, from floor to ceiling, was a dull white.

'How did I get here?' he asked. 'Where am I?' A clonk sounded and a skeleton emerged from a dark corner of the room, rattling.

The skeleton spoke. 'All rise.' Everyone in the room

stood up, including the worried Riley. Three tall, creepy ghosts with wrinkled faces entered the room. Moving mysteriously along the floor, they floated up behind a section of tiered white panelling then sat behind a word that Riley recognised. *JUDGES.*

The skeleton clonked forward a few steps. 'My lord ghosts, may I proceed with the first witness for the prosecution.' The skeleton waved his bony finger towards the audience of boys and girls – and beckoned the Slippery Geeks. They sneaked forward past the surprised Riley, who grumbled in disbelief. The mean-looking male ghost in the middle peered down at the Geeks.

'What do you have to say for yourselves?' he asked.

The Geeks looked up at his warped face then peeped to his left and right at the two straggly-haired female ghosts. 'We didn't do anything, sir,' replied one Geek. 'It's Riley – he's the bully. He picked on Daniel Brady and some other kids, and now he bosses us around all the time.'

The other Geek moved forward and spoke to the female ghost on the left. 'He tries to boss us around too. And his breath stinks. We just hang around him; we don't really like him.'

Riley jumped up from his seat, shouting, 'Creeps! Traitors!'

With that the middle ghost leaned forward, stretching his body across the room, shoving his wrinkles and warts to within centimetres of Riley's face. 'No one can see or hear you but us,' he snapped. 'We do not tolerate outbursts, so keep quiet.'

The old judge then waved his bony finger at the Geeks and they scurried back to their seats.

'The next witnesses, my noble ghosts,' rattled the skeleton, 'are two girls from the school who witnessed the bullying.'

The old female ghost on the right beckoned them towards her and then leaned forward, smiling. 'And what information can you two charming girls provide?' she asked.

One girl inched forward and gulped. 'I saw Riley kick and taunt Daniel Brady. Lots of boys and girls are frightened of him.'

The other girl stepped forward but dared not look up. 'I've seen Riley push Daniel Brady and call him names. There are lots of us who don't like Riley.'

The skeleton emerged once again, clonking across the floor. 'You may now be seated,' he said. The girls didn't hesitate. They ran back to their seats.

'My lord ghosts,' continued the skeleton. 'I call upon two teachers, Mr Shaw and Miss White, who witnessed the bullying.'

The skeleton beckoned Miss White and Mr Shaw forward.

'What can you tell us?' asked the old male ghost.

Mr Shaw glanced over the top of his glasses. 'Only recently have we witnessed Riley's cunning ways. He has attempted to deceive us with false information. He has told lies about Daniel Brady. We are concerned about him. We believe he may be a violent bully.'

Gasps and sighs rumbled through the courtroom.

'Silence!' ordered the skeleton.

The three judges turned to Miss White.

She shifted nervously then spoke hesitantly. 'Yes, I agree … yes, everything is true.'

The skeleton clonked forward once again. 'Please be seated. That concludes the case for the prosecution, my lord ghosts.'

'Are there any witnesses for the defence?' asked a female ghost.

Riley looked around hopefully, but everyone sat silent.

'There must be someone out there who can speak for the defence?' asked the ghost. She stretched her head forward, searching for someone to come forward, but there was no movement. The old male judge and the other female judge laughed grimly.

'I'll speak for him,' said a faint voice from the back. Gasps of surprise filled the room, followed by the mutter of voices as all eyes focused on Daniel Brady. He stood up, leaving Tyler and Sophie stunned. Boldly, he presented himself to the bench and stood before the friendly female ghost.

She leaned towards Daniel, smiling. 'Let us hear your plea, Daniel Brady, but tell the audience.'

Daniel faced Riley and the other pupils. 'Yes, it's true – Riley is a bully. We learn about bullies in school. Riley may have been bullied first. He may lack confidence, and his feelings have turned to anger. Or he could be afraid. A bully might be jealous, insecure or unhappy. Riley needs help. I'm sure there is some good in him. He can't be all bad – well, I hope not. Why is he a bully?'

The courtroom remained silent. Riley watched Daniel walk past him and sit down. The ghosts now moved closer together to discuss his case. But, to the annoyance of the male judge, the skeleton paced backward and forward, in front of the bench, until a decision was made.

The skeleton screeched: 'All rise.'

The old wiry ghost had decided. 'Do you have anything to say, Billy Riley, before I pass sentence?'

Riley could only utter the words, 'I'm sorry.'

'Billy Riley, the court finds you guilty of bullying. You will serve no less than three years in the reformatory.'

*'What?'* shrieked Riley. 'That's not fair.'

'All right then, five years!' roared the ghost. *Five years.* The words echoed in Riley's ears until … he yawned and opened his eyes.

'Oh God, it was only a nightmare,' Riley said, relieved. He sat up, looked around then screamed. 'Help me! Get me out of here!'

'What's the matter with you, Riley? 'Ad a bad dream, eh?' said a boy who lay on a bed next to him.

Riley didn't answer. He stared along the narrow room at the rows of scruffy kids sitting on battered beds. He touched his own bed. 'Have I been sitting on this grotty old thing?' he asked. 'There's straw poking out, and it smells like pee.'

'Peed on it, 'ave yer, Riley?' asked the same boy. 'My bed don't smell – can't say the same for Starver and Belter, though. They're real stinkers. Uh-oh, speak of the devil and they're sure to appear. Watch out, Riley, 'ere they come.'

Everyone dashed to their beds.

Riley lay focusing on two nasty-looking men dressed in stained black jackets with dishevelled hair. They mooched menacingly through the room past the foot of each bed. The taller one had a red face and swung a long buckled belt. The other man carried two buckets and stooped. His face was covered in scabs. They stopped near Riley's bed.

'Whose turn for a belting tonight?' bellowed the taller man, laughing. He glared around the room. 'My name's Mr Belter and you new 'uns should've already guessed what that means.'

The other coarse man set the buckets on the floor, spread his jacket then tugged at his braces. 'And if he don't belt yer to death I'll starve yer to death – cause my name's Mr Starver.'

Riley began to tremble. *I promise not to bully or steal any more. I don't belong here. Please, Mr Ghost, get me out of here.*

'Mostly thieves and troublemakers end up 'ere,' said Mr Starver. 'The boss says all new kids start on bread and water, so 'ere it is, in the buckets.'

The two men walked slyly past Riley and out of the door at the other end of the room.

'Phew, that's a relief,' Riley gasped, looking at the boy in the next bed.

'Keep still – stay on your bed,' warned the boy. Suddenly, a clatter of footsteps followed. Belter ran back in the room. Darting along by the beds, he grabbed a boy

141

standing near the buckets.

'Gotcha, yer you little rascal,' he scowled. 'Who said yer' could eat and drink?' He lifted the belt and struck the boy with all his might. Time and time again he strapped the boy's backside, swinging his powerful arms back and forth. Riley cowered with fright, but part of him wanted to jump from the bed and stop the crazed man. The boy in the next bed signalled to Riley.

'Shush,' he whispered, placing a finger to his lips.

Riley then stared at the ugly moving shadow of Belter spread across the candlelit wall.

'Please, Mr Ghost,' he whispered. 'Take me back. I'll be good.'

In a flash, the ghost stood by Riley's bed. He scowled.

'Is that a promise? Are you sure?'

Riley nodded.

'Then come with me,' said the ghost, clutching at him and lifting him up. He took Riley and vanished.

Riley groaned and opened his eyes. He looked nervously all around before jumping out of bed. 'This is my bedroom, isn't it? It looks real. God, that was a nasty dream.'

He touched his bed, then dived to the window and heaved a sigh of relief. He flung back the curtain, shouting, 'Yes, yes, it's my room! I'm back! Quick, where's Daniel's chain? I've got to give it back to him.'

He ran back to his bed, throwing the pillow on the floor. 'Chain, where are you?' He caught sight of something glittering on the floor. He dived down, picked it up and dropped it in his rucksack. 'Got it – what a relief.'

# Chapter 17

That day, Riley waited for the right moment. 'Miss Tubble,' he said, 'I found this chain near the sports field.'

She held out her chubby fingers. 'Well done, Riley – honesty is the best policy.' She peered closely at the chain. 'This is unusual; I wonder who it belongs to.'

'I don't know,' Riley replied, shivering. 'And I don't care.' At that moment a chill wind blew around Middleton High. Leaves swirled in clusters, rustling along the empty playground. A whistling sound reverberated throughout the school and dark shadows crept mysteriously over the rooftops. One by one the lights in the corridors and classrooms dimmed and flickered. Everyone in the school listened to the eerie sounds – including Riley, who had also spotted a skeleton standing nearby. He quickly turned and bumped straight into Miss Griffin, knocking a bundle of papers from her hands.

'You silly boy!' she shouted. 'Why are you running? Anyone would think you had seen a ghost.'

'S-sorry, Miss,' he stuttered, scrabbling around on the floor, picking up her papers. 'But I did! There's a skeleton back there.'

'What on earth are you talking about, Billy Riley?'

'It's along the corridor, Miss – somewhere,' he said, handing her the papers and running off.

'What's up with Billy Riley?' asked Miss Griffin.

'I don't know,' replied Miss Tubble. 'But have a look at this.'

Miss Griffin gaped at the chain. 'Ooh, that's a nice piece of jewellery – looks expensive.'

'Doesn't it just. Billy Riley handed it to me.'

The howling wind continued. It made the windows rattle. Frightened pupils gathered in groups everywhere.

'What's that strange noise?' asked Miss Griffin.

Miss Tubble cupped her hand behind her ear. 'Sounds like a rattling metal lid. I can hear clanking.' Her hair began to stand on end as the sound came closer. She screamed, dropping the chain. 'Something hot just touched my hand.'

'I just thought I saw...' Miss Griffin paused. 'Something whizzing past us.'

'Don't be silly now, ladies,' remarked Mr Shaw, who happened to be walking past. 'Next you'll be thinking it was me flying along the corridor. We should be calming the pupils, not frightening them. Enough strange things are happening around here without you two scaremongering. You two know the school is supposed to be haunted – and you know about the prophecy. We don't want this gossip spread around.'

Miss Griffin swayed. 'Ooh, I feel faint.'

'Me too,' sighed Miss Tubble, holding her forehead and trembling. 'I think we should sit down.'

'What's this on the floor?' asked Mr Shaw, picking

up the chain.

'Lost property,' replied Miss Tubble. 'I dropped it. Could you take it Mr Shaw and hand it in?'

'Okay, I'm going that way. Ladies, I'll see you both later. Don't forget, rehearsals are on tonight for the Christmas play.'

Miss Tubble waited for Mr Shaw to walk away, then spoke. 'I feel uneasy.'

Miss Griffin was busy looking at her reflection in the window. 'Everyone's on edge around here.'

'You can say that again,' replied Miss Tubble.

That afternoon the wind continued to howl around the school and lights flickered. Creepy sounds whisked around every corner of the building, fading only when home time approached. Boys and girls scurried along the corridors, eager to leave.

Miss Griffin's voice echoed throughout the corridor. 'Don't forget – all those in the Christmas play report to the main hall, immediately.'

'Scene two, take one,' barked a bossy sixth-form girl. Daniel, Sophie and Tyler stood on stage in their white sheets and hoods, peeping through tiny slits.

'You didn't tell us we were going to be crappy old ghosts,' said Tyler.

'Sorry. I didn't know,' Daniel replied.

'I don't mind,' Sophie said. 'This could be fun. It's better than scary dreams, anyway.'

They all raised their arms in the air and waited for Mr Shaw to call out his instructions.

'You three ghosts,' said Mr Shaw, 'lean slightly forward, as if you're ready to pounce on the wicked baron. Let's dim the lights for this scene.' Faintly, the stage dimmed, leaving a small pool of light shimmering across the old wooden four-poster bed that stood on stage. Artificial moonlight shone through a small leaded window that lit up an old wardrobe, alongside a large painting that hung, crooked, on the wall. Eerie music played while the three ghosts, Daniel, Tyler and Sophie, crept quietly across the stage, heading towards the sleeping baron.

Mr Shaw casually observed the scene along with a few others sitting near to the stage. He put his hand in his pocket, then realised he still had the chain.

'Oh damn,' he said. 'I forgot to hand this in.'

At that moment, a fourth ghost darted across the floor of the stage.

'What was that?' asked Mr Shaw. 'Did I see something? Or is the light playing tricks?'

'I didn't see anything,' replied Miss White, sitting next to him. Daniel, Sophie or Tyler hadn't seen anything on stage either and carried on as normal, moving around the baron's bed, waving their arms like ghosts.

'You go first, Tyler,' Daniel whispered. 'I'm next, and then Sophie – got it.' One by one the three ghosts dropped through the stage trapdoor and disappeared under the stage.

Mr Shaw praised them. 'Cut, everyone. Very good.'

All three stooped under the stage and pulled their hoods off.

'It's too hot,' complained Sophie, 'especially underneath here.'

Tyler pointed at the dark corners. 'Anything could be lurking here.'

Daniel pushed them aside. 'You two are such wimps.' He led the way under the stage through a row of fairy lights and emerged backstage. They scrambled out of the small door and mingled with the other actors and actresses, who were busy preparing for the next scene.

'Well done, you three,' commented Miss Tubble.

'Yes, well done,' added Miss Griffin. 'You acted just like real ghosts.'

'Did any of you hear anything strange on stage?' asked Miss Tubble.

Daniel smirked. 'I saw a sixth former dressed up as an old baron, Miss.'

'And he was in bed laughing,' added Tyler.

'He didn't like us, Miss,' grumbled Sophie. 'He said we were all creeps and he told us to push off, or else.'

'Oh, did he now?'

'Come here, you three,' beckoned Miss Griffin. 'Stand side by side; let's have a couple of photos.' She pushed them together, stood back and took the picture. 'Now put your hoods on.'

They all obliged and she went to take another snap, but stopped. 'What in heaven's name was that?' she asked, lowering the camera. 'I thought something flashed across the lens.' But no one answered, so she took the picture and at the same time a skeleton appeared by Tyler's side, then rapidly vanished.

'D-did you see *that?*' Miss Griffin asked again.

Miss Tubble rubbed her eyes. 'I saw *something*, but I'm not sure what.'

Miss Griffin began nosing around. 'Did anyone else see that?'

A few boys and girls shook their heads. At that moment Mr Shaw walked past.

'Now where can I put this?' he said, swinging a life-sized skeleton directly in front of Miss Griffin.

She jumped out of her skin. 'Mr Shaw, you frightened me; did you have to do that?'

'Do what?' he asked, turning to speak to Daniel. 'You three – off you go and get ready for your next scene.'

'Do you think we look scary, sir?' asked Sophie.

Tyler held up his arms. 'We're the ghost dusters, sir.'

Mr Shaw laughed. 'Off you go.'

'Remember what I told you,' said Daniel, 'when it gets to winter. Some nasty things happen around here. The teachers go ballistic, witches and wizards fight, and—'

'I just saw a shadow,' interrupted Sophie, 'creep past the window.'

'Stop imagining things,' said Daniel. 'You scare too easily.'

Riley and the Geeks crouched outside the window, peering in.

'Stay out of sight,' Riley whispered. 'We'll get them backstage.' He then thought about the ghost and the chain, wondering if it had been a dream. 'You two wouldn't split on me, would you?'

Both Geeks shook their heads.

'I mean, we are still friends, aren't we?'

The Geeks held up their thumbs and nodded.

'You weren't in front of three judges recently, were you?'

The Geeks fidgeted, without answering.

Riley thought for a few seconds. 'Oh forget that. Anyway, what's going on in there?' He peered in through the window. 'Look, there's Brady – let's try and spoil a few things.'

There came a *WHOOSH* from behind them.

'What was that?' asked Riley nervously.

All three spun around, looking beyond the playground into the darkness. Nothing stirred apart from the sound of distant traffic.

'That noise sounded a bit scary. Do you two believe in ghosts?'

The Geeks looked all around, worried.

'Forget what I said; let's just get Brady.'

They peered back into the hall.

'What a bunch of nerds,' sneered Riley, 'in a crappy old play.'

But the Geeks weren't looking in the hall. They were mesmerised by a reflection in the window, and dare not move. A wrinkly, mean-looking face flickered in the glass. The Geeks edged sideways, bumping into Riley.

'Don't push me,' complained Riley.

'B-b-but—' mumbled one Geek.

Riley turned and glared at him. 'What's the matter?

149

Scared of the dark, are we?'

The Geeks signalled for Riley to look behind him.

He looked. 'What?' he retorted. 'There's nothing there.'

But the Geeks had seen enough. They turned and ran. They darted around the school buildings, with Riley in hot pursuit.

'Stop, stop, it's okay,' pleaded Riley.

The Geeks eventually came to a halt, puffing and panting. Riley buckled at the knees, gasping for air. 'What's the matter with you two?' he asked, coughing. 'Can't you take a joke?'

The Geeks weren't laughing. Then one spoke. 'A ghost – we saw a ghost.'

Then the other Geek whinged, 'We're not kidding.'

Riley was edgy. 'You were tricked.'

The Geeks stared into the darkness of the playing fields as Riley wiped the sweat from his forehead.

'Look,' he said, 'there's nothing out there, trust me.' He then beckoned them to follow. 'Let's see if the stage door is open.'

They crept along the dark pathway, making their way back to the hall. The cold night air drifted up around their faces. Riley led the way. The unlit solid door at the rear of the stage stood before them. Riley walked up the three steps and grabbed the handle.

He pulled the door towards him, ogling through the gap, then smiled. 'Just what I want,' he whispered, opening the door further. He crept in while the Geeks kept watch. Within seconds he strolled back outside, carrying something white. 'What d'ya reckon, then?' he joked, closing the stage door and pulling a ghost costume over his head. 'Scary?' He came back slowly down the steps. 'Whoo – whoo – real scary, eh?'

The Geeks weren't amused. To make matters worse, they had seen a strange white image moving alongside Riley. He was swaying sideways, messing about, pretending to be a ghost, groaning.

They watched the white image beginning to mirror Riley's movements. The Geeks froze. Riley and his white shadow came towards them.

'What's the matter?' asked Riley. 'Seen another ghost, have we? You two scared?'

Then a face formed in the white image and the ghost mimicked the same words. 'What's the matter? Seen another ghost, have we? You two scared?'

Riley laughed. 'Which one of you two said that?'

The Geeks didn't speak. They just stumbled away. Riley laughed again, clowning around even more. The Geeks shuffled away, then turned heel and ran.

'Wait! Stop,' called Riley. 'Anyone would think you've seen a real ghost.' He chased after the Geeks, removing the ghost costume as he ran. 'Come back! Wait.' But the Geeks ran past the school buildings into the playground before disappearing out of the school gates. Riley finally stopped running and bent forward, panting. 'What's up with them two?' he croaked, puffing.

'What's up with them two?' came the echo.

'Who said that?' asked Riley.

'Who said that?'

Riley looked up at a shadowy image, then screamed. He ran back to the safety of the school building – and ran headlong into Miss Griffin.

'What on earth are you doing here?'

'Um, um, someone said there were rehearsals, Miss.'

'I didn't know you were in the play, Billy Riley.'

'Nor did I, Miss, but someone said an extra might be needed.'

'We'll soon find out. Follow me.'

The rehearsals were in full swing.

'What's Riley up to now?' asked Sophie, tapping Daniel on the shoulder. 'He's in the hall – look over there.'

'Forget him,' replied Daniel. 'We've got more important things to do.'

Tyler rolled his eyes. 'Yeah, man, we're the ghost dusters.'

Miss Griffin discussed the possibility of including Riley in the play with Mr Shaw and Miss White. 'Looks like we may fit you in somewhere, Billy,' she said. 'Sit here with Mr Shaw.'

'Thanks, Miss,' replied Riley, reluctant to sit next to any teacher – especially Mr Shaw, who had been probing and asking too many questions.

Rehearsals resumed. Mr Shaw sat next to Miss White, directing the play. But he soon became distracted. 'Can you hear something?'

Miss White continued to concentrate on the play. 'Can I hear what?'

'I'm not sure – perhaps it's my imagination.' Mr Shaw scratched his head. 'There it goes again.'

He heard a rattle, as if someone was dragging a heavy chain across the ground.

Miss White heard it too. 'That's an excellent sound effect.'

Mr Shaw glanced around. 'I didn't organise that noise.'

Billy Riley heard the chain too and stood up smartly. 'Please, sir, sir, I need to visit the toilet, sir.' Riley didn't wait for an answer from Mr Shaw; he scurried off out of the hall.

Mr Shaw inspected the sound system while the play continued. 'That's strange,' he said. 'I can still hear chains rattling and it seems to be getting louder. Where on earth is the noise coming from?'

He went backstage and inspected every piece of equipment. He pulled a tissue from his pocket to wipe his forehead. Daniel's chain fell from his pocket, unnoticed, and hit the floor with a chink. 'That's strange,' he said. 'The noise has stopped. Oh, well, everyone, get ready for the next scene.' He called to Daniel. 'That includes you three, even though I'm not sure about ghosts on stage tonight.'

'Has someone dropped a chain?' a girl asked, picking it up.

Daniel's eyes lit up when he saw the shiny chain dangling from her fingers. 'It's mine!' he exclaimed.

But things were moving fast.

'On stage, you three ghosts,' called the prompt.

153

Daniel held out his hand, trying to reach his chain, but Miss Tubble pushed him forward onto the stage.

'She's got my chain, Miss,' he complained.

'Shush, too late,' replied Sophie. 'We're on stage.'

All three crept around the stage but Daniel wasn't concentrating. They ducked in and out of the light, hiding in the shadows, looking scary. They sauntered around the baron's bedroom, taunting him. Then one by one they moved towards the trapdoor.

'Did you see that?' whispered Daniel. 'Someone else is on stage, dressed like a ghost.'

'We know,' replied Tyler. 'He is a ghostly-looking baron pretending to be asleep.'

'No, seriously,' Daniel whispered. 'I just saw it again.'

'I didn't see anything,' replied Sophie.

As before, they walked down the steps beneath the stage, emerging into the dressing area backstage.

'It's becoming a bit spooky in here,' claimed Daniel, looking for the girl and his chain. 'Where is she?'

Suddenly the stage door sprang open. Outside, the wind howled. Everyone stopped, wondering what had happened. They watched nervously as Daniel walked towards the shiny chain, which dangled, suspended in mid-air, in the middle of the doorway. He held out his hand and the chain mysteriously drifted towards him. The shiny link of hands trailed neatly around his neck and snapped shut.

# Chapter 18

December arrived, bringing with it colder weather. Damp air penetrated through the older houses in the city and the Brady family needed the central heating at full blast to keep warm. Daniel held Chip in his arms and stroked his warm body.

'It's nice and snug in here, Chip. We're lucky; it must have been a lot worse a hundred years ago, or a thousand. I bet there were ghosts around then as well.'

Chip's ears pricked up as Daniel's mum knocked on the bedroom door. 'Can I come in? How was the play rehearsal? Not too scary, I hope?'

'No, Mum. It was tame, considering.'

'Considering what?'

'Considering the scary things I've seen.'

'A new school can be a bit scary. You have been there for a while, so it should be getting better.'

'You could say that.'

'Goodnight, and don't forget we want three tickets for the school play.'

Daniel was soon tucked up in bed, stroking Chip, thinking about the old castle and manor. 'I wonder why the school has secrets buried in its walls, Chip. And who is Buddy Wizard? Who was he when he was alive?

Where did he come from?'

Chip wagged his tail. Daniel closed his eyes. Together they fell peacefully asleep.

The next morning Daniel met Tyler and Sophie in the playground.

'I think the teachers may know this school could be haunted,' Daniel remarked.

Sophie laughed. 'What makes you think that?'

'They know all about its history. We need to look outside in the garden area again.'

'No chance,' replied Tyler.

Sophie threw her arms in the air. 'No! You go if you want.'

However, they reluctantly joined Daniel along the north corridor to the crossover link, with Daniel deep in thought, gazing out of the window.

'Something strange is happening to me,' Daniel said, twisting the chain around his fingers. 'I can see the walls of the old castle.'

'Where?' asked Sophie, stopping.

Daniel closed his eyes and pointed. 'The wall is there.'

Tyler frowned at the thought. 'He's heading to the courtyard garden. Let's get out of here.'

But Daniel seemed to be in a trance. He began to walk towards the exit door.

Sophie grabbed his arm, trying to pull him back. 'Daniel, stop – please stop.'

Tyler ran in front of Daniel. 'Wake up! Quick, wake up.' But Daniel ignored them and carried on walking.

Soon they had attracted the attention of other boys and girls, who stopped to see what was happening.

'Do something, Tyler,' begged Sophie.

The bewildered Tyler created a diversion. He ran past the onlookers to the other side of the crossover link, jumping up and waving his arms. 'Look, everyone,' he said, trying to attract their attention. All of the kids took notice – except one person, who wasn't fooled. Billy Riley had his eyes fixed firmly on Daniel. He watched him push past Sophie, walk into the garden to the statue figure and touch it.

Riley's eyes bulged when he saw Daniel vanish. 'Miss Tubble, come quickly! Daniel Brady has gone.'

Daniel stood in the cold, dark grounds of the old manor, listening to dogs barking in the distance. He looked ahead at the creepy old building and felt compelled to venture there once again. He made his way along the dark pathway to the old manor, peering at the small lights flickering in the windows. He approached the old front door. It stretched up, looking like a dark monster ready to growl. He pushed the huge door but it wouldn't budge. The barking grew louder. Daniel panicked, ran to the side of the building and began forcing his way through the bushes. He slid his hand along the stone wall, not knowing where it would lead. The prickly undergrowth clawed at his hands and face as he struggled to feel his way through the brambles. What's this? he thought, feeling an opening. He stumbled against a door, leaned and pushed with all his might. The door creaked and partly opened. He squeezed through the narrow opening as the howling and barking grew near. Hastily, he forced the door shut.

It was dark. Daniel slid his hands along the mottled surface of the wall. A gentle breeze stroked his cheeks and his eyes watered. He sensed the eeriness of the tunnel, and headed for a faint light in the distance. Daniel moved cautiously. The light rebounded off the walls and grew stronger. He turned into a corridor lined by a row of glowing candles that flickered, revealing the way ahead. He began to see eerie eyes, like those that hung in the school corridors of Middleton High.

*Whoosh!*

'So you have returned?' said a loud voice. Daniel watched the ghostly figure that hovered above him. The white, distorted face of Miss Griffin glared at him and she laughed grimly.

Daniel held up his arm for protection then looked closer at her face. 'You're not Miss Griffin – you're a witch.'

'I'm a Punisher,' she screamed. 'I punish those that are brought here.' She then disappeared into the distance. Daniel instinctively ran along the candlelit corridor then darted through a doorway.

A sinister voice screamed out, 'You're not welcome here!'

Daniel cringed at the ghostly face covered in warts. It looked like Miss Tubble.

'You as well – you're not Miss Tubble either. You're both witches.' Daniel cowered away then ran along the passage away from them. He heard the sound of running water and cautiously approached the noise. The sound grew louder and louder. Daniel stumbled upon a stream running fast under the passageway. He became spellbound by the glistening water below him.

'Come closer,' said a nearby voice. Warily, Daniel stepped back. A figure emerged from the shadows. 'Come and take a look,' the voice said.

Daniel strained to see clearly. He made out a face that looked like Mr North – but it was ashen and worn. He knew it wasn't Mr North.

'I'm one of the Punishers,' Mr North chuckled. 'And the bullies go in the river.'

Daniel ran away, then hid in the shadows shaking. He could feel something touch him.

'Do you want to return home?' said a voice.

Daniel did a double take. 'Buddy Wizard, it's you! Thank God.'

'You are not safe here,' said Buddy Wizard. 'There are angry ghosts lurking – come with me.'

They carried on along the creepy passage into a large hall. There were high vertical windows through which shone slivers of light. Cobwebs hung from the overhead beams. Buddy Wizard waved his hand and a sprinkling of stars flew around them. 'This is the hall of judgement, Daniel,' said Buddy Wizard. 'You must stay silent.' Suddenly, a ghost entered the hall. Then others followed: ghosts of men, women and children dressed in rags. Some muttered words of revenge. Daniel was wide-eyed and trembling as the ghosts surrounded him and Buddy Wizard.

Daniel edged closer to Buddy Wizard. 'What's happening here?'

The ghosts sat in a small arena, their gaunt faces eager.

'Why are they not looking at us?' asked Daniel.

'We are in a different time zone,' said Buddy Wizard. 'They cannot see you. They know of your presence but cannot harm you. You are witnessing the past judgement of tormentors, bullies, and those that sent the poor and innocent to their graves.'

All heads turned to see three elderly ghosts enter at the end of the great room.

The middle ghost beckoned the guards. 'Bring forth the accused!'

'He's scary,' said Daniel. Five wicked men stood facing the mean-looking judges.

'Were they punished?'

'You will see,' answered the boy ghost.

The wiry old male ghost grimaced at the culprits. He craned his neck to look more closely at the men. 'We can all see you now,' he remarked. 'You are guilty.' The old lady judge to the left scowled and asked them why they had all chosen to persecute others. One by one the men gave feeble excuses.

'Burn them at the stake, like I was!' screamed a voice.

'Torture them on the rack, like I was!' yelled another.

'Drown them, like I was!'

'Torment them and feed them to the rats!'

'Give them a taste of their own medicine!'

'Haunt them forever!'

The lady judge on the right threw her hands up in the air. The walls shook. 'Have you no pity?' she asked. 'Even after many years have passed, you still seek revenge.'

A grumbling of discontent followed.

'We will rely on the test,' the male judge said. 'Your vote will determine the fate of these.'

The men stood huddled together, cowering.

'Show us your vote for punishment one,' dictated the male judge.

'What's punishment one?' asked Daniel.

'Be patient – you will see.'

'All those who wish to vote for punishment one, raise your hand, then depart,' said the lady judge. She counted the show of hands. The remaining ghosts then voted for punishment two and departed from the hall.

'What are the punishments?' asked Daniel.

Buddy Wizard hesitated to answer. 'Just pray it is punishment three.' The accused men peeked through their sunken eyes, bewildered, repentant, knowing their fate was in the hands of the ghosts. The ghosts raised their hands for punishment three.

'I don't like the look of those ugly ghost judges,' Daniel whispered. 'The straggly-haired one looks dangerous.'

'You mean my mother?' replied Buddy.

'She's your mum? S-s-sorry. Can't we just go?' asked Daniel. 'I'm getting scared.'

'No, the result is near.'

161

The ghosts returned to the hall, waiting to hear the result.

'The punishment is two,' called Buddy Wizard's mother. Many of the ghosts started to grumble.

'Some will be angry,' said Buddy Wizard. 'They chose punishment one – death. This could spell trouble.'

He touched Daniel and they immediately disappeared into the lower building, through the candlelit maze of passageways – and once again to the wall of the clasped hands.

'You should not return to this place, Daniel. My mother has tried for centuries to influence those who have awakened from the crypts, and to educate those who only seek revenge on their tormentors. Many poor, innocent people have been persecuted as witches and wizards. All the ghosts you see here were once people. They were all bullied or murdered. Mother and I were part of a family of farmers. We were known as field stumpers. This included my father, three brothers and two sisters. I was the youngest. From the age of six I would scare the birds away from crops, sow potatoes, look after animals and collect firewood. After three years I learned to plough our land, tend to the horses, clean the stables and look after the pigs. We were doing well – until the landowner accused us of pilfering, witchcraft and blasphemy. My family were bullied and tortured. All their possessions were taken … and finally we were all killed – except my mother and me. She pleaded for my life. I was sent to Middleton Manor Orphanage. Mother died of heartache. I ran away from the orphanage, married and was put to death aged sixteen – a month before my wife was due to have our baby.'

'In the beginning, we all craved revenge. However, often we tried to meet the living, only a few of us succeeded. Most slept through the ages until their rage awoke them again. Many now seek a different punishment. But, be warned – not all ghosts seek the same punishment.'

'I can hear footsteps,' Daniel said. 'This is not a dream. Someone is coming.'

Two familiar figures emerged from the shadows. They seemed in a trance, gawking at Buddy Wizard.

'Now look,' said Mr North, 'we got sucked through the wall looking for Brady. Where is he?'

Riley answered. 'I don't know, Mr North.'

Daniel looked more closely at Mr North then circled nervously behind Buddy Wizard. 'It is really Mr North. Riley must have convinced Mr North to go to the courtyard to look for me.'

'They are in a spell,' said Buddy Wizard. 'One of the Punishers must have entered the school and tricked them into venturing here. If they have that means others could enter.'

'What about Mr North and Riley?' asked Daniel. 'They're going the wrong way. There's a room full of ghosts there.'

'Master Riley needs another lesson – and we will follow,' said Buddy Wizard.

Daniel knew he had found a secret passageway to Middleton Castle. The grey walls of the fortress surrounded him with its shiny armour and shields. He strode on, recognising the school plaque that gave him comfort and hope. His eyes fixed on the last few words. *Your strength that has carried you this far can take you the rest of the way.*

Mr North and Riley descended along the passageway into a tunnel which turned into a wider passage, Buddy Wizard and Daniel following discreetly.

'Stay near me, Daniel,' said Buddy. 'We must take care from here on.'

Daniel and Buddy entered the gloomy passage, which led to a wider opening with rows of wooden cages on either side. The cages were two metres square and built of sturdy wooden poles, spaced just far enough apart to see through. Water trickled along a crooked gutter in the middle of the large passage.

Daniel held his nose as a rat scurried past. This place is nasty, he thought, and it smells like the toilets in the school. They heard groaning coming from the cages, and rustling. Daniel cringed. 'What types of animals are kept here?'

Buddy Wizard walked towards a cage. 'This is where the Punishers keep their prey.'

Daniel peered through the gaps. 'What sort of prey?'

'Human prey,' replied Buddy.

*'What?'* shrieked Daniel, leaping back from the cage.

'Humans are kept here before they go to trial.'

Daniel gulped then asked, 'For how long?'

'For as long as the Punishers wish.'

'That's cruel.'

'Yes, it is cruel, Daniel – even for some of the nastiest bullies.' Buddy Wizard passed by the cages, beckoning Daniel to move on. 'It would appear some Punishers are now bullies.'

They looked in the cages that had their doors open, but others were securely barred and groans came from within.

'So much has changed here, but there is still more to do. The Punishers struggle to forgive and don't see the need for change.'

They reached the last cages. Beyond, stood a dark doorway.

'There are lots of cages,' said Daniel. 'But most are empty.'

'Be quiet, Daniel. I fear the Punishers are near: you must go into this cage quickly.'

However, it was Riley and Mr North who emerged from the darkness and stared at Daniel in the cage.

'I would rather be in here,' said Daniel. 'Take a look behind you.'

'We're not falling for that, are we, Mr North?'

But the ghostly witches who resembled Miss Griffin and Miss Tubble towered above Riley, peering down at him disapprovingly. Daniel hastily flinched away from the bars, eager to distance himself from them. Buddy Wizard smiled as they lifted Riley off his feet.

'Hey, put me down,' Riley said, wriggling. But in a flash they had put him in a cage and slid the bar across.

The ghosts burst into hideous laughter and left. 'We have another bad 'un in the cage.'

Mr North looked bewildered.

Riley groaned. 'Let me out of here.'

Daniel wiped his forehead. 'The ghosts look like my teachers again.'

'No, Daniel, they are Punishers fooling you again. We must leave here.'

'What about Mr North and Riley?'

But Buddy Wizard ignored Daniel. In a twinkling of stars they disappeared.

The ghostly Punishers flew back along the rows of cages, hovering menacingly around Mr North. Their faces stretched and twisted, changing their appearance. 'It is unfortunate we cannot accommodate Mr North here,' commented one ghost.

'But continue being nasty,' said the other ghost, 'and we will get you.' They moved closer to the wooden bars. 'We will soon have more bullies like you.' Riley jumped back as the ghosts rushed off, laughing again.

'Mr North, can you hear me?' asked Riley.

Mr North only shuffled his feet.

'I'm over here – behind you.' Riley beckoned.

Mr North ignored him. Riley called again. 'Here in this cage,'

But Mr North lurched away. Furiously, Riley grabbed the bars. 'You idiot, can't you hear me?'

But Mr North didn't speak. Riley gripped the bars more tightly. 'I'm here.' Mr North stumbled along the uneven passageway. Riley pushed his face into the bars sideways. 'Come back, you moron.' He turned away, frustrated, then sat dejected on the straw. Only a few minutes had passed when Riley heard a noise. He jumped up.

'Who's there?' he asked apprehensively. He put his ear to the bar. 'It sounds like someone dragging something.' The noise came closer. Riley forced his hand through the narrow bars and tried in vain to touch Mr North, now dragging one foot along the floor.

'Help me, Mr North – get me out of here.' But Mr North ignored him and headed back the other way. Riley grabbed hold of the bars, shouting, 'Come back, you zombie.'

Mr North shuffled past Riley time and time again. Riley shouted at him in vain until he finally gave up.

'Why am I locked up?' Riley asked. 'I don't like it here. It's all Brady's fault.' And with that, four small ghosts appeared. Riley edged away from the bars and covered his eyes, trembling.

A girl spoke. 'We want to help you.'

Riley opened his eyes to see four blue silhouettes of children ogling him.

'We were locked up too,' said a girl.

'We were all bullied,' said another.

Then the small boy asked, 'Are you repentant?'

Riley puckered his eyebrows, confused. He didn't answer, but instead asked, 'Where have you all come from?'

The three girls each replied:

'We live here.'

'We help Buddy.'

'Buddy says we are the saviours. We try to save

people like you, but the elders do not always agree.'

'Please let me go,' said Riley.

Just then, a roar echoed through the passageway and a mean-looking ghost appeared. The young ghosts scampered away into the gloom. Riley leaned against the bars, sobbing. 'Please let me out,' he cried. 'I wanna go home.' He bowed his head, closed his eyes and sat down.

A couple of hours rolled by, then a voice whispered, 'Billy Riley, I have come to take you home.'

Riley jumped to his feet but couldn't see anyone. The cage door swung open and he panicked. He ran out of the cage, shouting, and didn't stop until Buddy Wizard pointed a beam of light at him and lifted him off his feet, his legs dangling.

'Put me back down,' Riley shouted. 'Help me!'

Daniel, Mr North and Riley followed Buddy Wizard in a stream of light. They went up the stairway, along corridors, around corners, past flickering candles, until they reached the carvings on the wall, next to an archway between two statues.

'You must go through there,' said Buddy Wizard, pointing to the archway. 'The Punishers will be angry with me for releasing Billy Riley.'

They passed through the arch. Rays of light shone out, and in the blink of an eye they vanished.

Daniel appeared in the courtyard first. He ran from the garden into the school. He looked back through the window, waiting to see if Mr North and Riley had also returned.

'What are you looking at?' asked a voice from behind

Daniel.

'I'm looking for Riley,' Daniel said, without thinking. He then looked out of the corner of his eye, wondering who asked him. He spotted a face next to his and shot away from the window. 'Argh! It's you, Miss Griffin.'

She towered above Daniel. 'Well, you won't find him out there,' she replied. 'Run along – you can't hang around here.'

Daniel walked away, still looking for Riley.

Billy Riley reappeared in the courtyard, along with Mr North. Miss Griffin blinked twice in disbelief. She turned to say something, but Daniel had dodged off out of sight.

Sophie shuddered when Daniel told them what had happened.

'We believe you, Daniel, don't we Tyler?'

'Yeah – looks like the prophecy is coming true now, doesn't it? So what do we do? Who do we tell?'

'I don't know,' answered Daniel. 'Who would believe us?'

# Chapter 19

The weekend passed without incident. On Monday Daniel, Sophie and Tyler were in the science room.

'Look at that skull,' said Daniel. 'It's smiling at you, Sophie.' They all peered at a plastic skeleton, which seemed to stare back.

'Stop joking,' replied Sophie. 'I don't like skeletons or ghosts. I asked my mum if she thinks ghosts exist. She just smiled, gave me a hug and said not to be silly. I was going to ask my dad, but he'll say the same. He thinks I'm still eight.'

'You don't have to worry. Ghosts only go after bullies.'

Tyler wiped his forehead. 'Thank God.'

'Buddy Wizard is a friendly ghost. The others are ghost Punishers. They're the scary ones. I even got scared, Sophie.'

They strolled up to the reception area, where the tall Christmas tree stood with its colourful decorations and lights. They gazed at the tinsel that hung from the tree's branches, each of them wondering what would happen next.

'It's only two weeks to Christmas,' Sophie said. 'I hope everything will be okay.'

'Who cares?' scoffed Riley, walking past. 'You won't get away with it, Brady.'

'Get away with what, Riley?'

'Making things up and trying to scare people.'

'Are you scared of ghosts?'

Riley chuckled. 'Who said I'm scared of ghosts?'

'Buddy Wizard.'

'Who's he?' Riley asked, smirking.

'A ghost,' said Daniel. Sophie and Tyler tried to pull Daniel away, but to no avail – and it didn't take long for a small audience to gather.

'A ghost, eh?' asked Riley, laughing. 'You know a ghost, do you? Listen, everyone – Brady knows a ghost.'

The boys and girls had started to make ghost noises. In the confusion, Sophie and Tyler slipped discreetly away.

The gathering had also attracted Mr North. 'Stop that noise at once,' he demanded. 'What's going on?'

Riley answered without thinking. 'I found a silver chain sir and handed it in. Brady said it belongs to him.'

'Is that true, Daniel Brady?'

'Yes sir, it's mine.'

'Where did you get it from, then?'

Daniel thought on his feet. 'It was a present.'

'From who?'

'A relative.'

'What relative?'

'I'm not sure – my uncle.'

Mr North held out his hand. 'Look, Brady, I'm confiscating the chain until we find out the truth. Don't worry, Daniel. If it is yours you'll get it back.'

Mr North looked puzzled, holding his chin. 'Also, I seem to recall some strange things happening around here.'

Daniel unfastened the link and placed the chain in Mr North's hand. But as he did so, Mr North tossed the chain up in the air. 'Ouch! It's hot!'

All the kids laughed as he danced around, fumbling with the chain, until Mr North quickly wrapped it in his handkerchief and stuffed it in his pocket. 'Right!' he snapped, red-faced. 'Everyone, get back to your classes.'

Daniel glared angrily at Riley. The other kids all strolled past him, laughing.

'We tried to pull you away,' said Sophie.

'You wouldn't listen.'

'I made a fool of myself; Mr North's got my chain.'

Tyler clenched his fist. 'Riley needs to be taught a lesson.'

'Yeah, by Buddy Wizard,' said Sophie. 'Oops, sorry, Daniel,' she added, placing her hand over her mouth.

That evening Daniel lay in bed with Chip nestling against his feet. 'I think Riley is jealous of me, Chip. He thinks he can do anything. He doesn't realise he's the one with the problem. No one really likes him.'

Chip flicked his ears then exhaled noisily, which made Daniel yawn.

'I know who has the answer, Chip. Buddy Wizard.'

It was quiet in the Brady household, except for the odd creak of floorboards. Daniel was missing his chain, thinking of ways to get his own back on Riley. It was around midnight, and unusually dark, when a light penetrated Daniel's eyes. Confused, he sat up in bed.

'Sorry, Daniel,' said his dad, standing over him. 'I thought I heard something.'

'I heard something too,' whispered Emily, following him. 'It sounded like wind whistling.'

Mr Brady checked all around the room. 'It must be the central heating pipes. They've been a bit odd lately. Oh well, back to bed, everyone.'

The lights went off and Daniel lay awake.

'Chip – come here, boy,' Daniel whispered. Chip snuggled up to him, wagging his tail. 'I think that's a sign Buddy Wizard was here, Chip. Did you hear him? I hope he gets Riley tonight.'

\*\*\*

Billy Riley lay in bed, thinking. *Perhaps I should have told Mr North the truth about Daniel's chain. What the hell? I'm not bothered.* He then thought about the night he had scared Daniel and his friends in the tent. He chuckled, remembering Chip trying to catch him and the Geeks. He laughed about the tricks he had played on kids and ones he wanted to play in future. Then he became sombre. He remembered the dream he'd had about a ghost following him, waiting for him to fall asleep. When he did fall asleep, he had his worst nightmare yet.

'Who's there?' mumbled Riley. 'Leave me alone.'

He pulled the bed covers over his head. The bedroom lit up, revealing a dark mist. He peeked out from under the bed covers, only to see a shadow gathering and forming around a dark shape. The ghost floated to where Riley lay. He glared fiercely at Riley with piercing green eyes.

'Billy Riley,' said the ghost, 'I am the Ghost of Future Children.'

Riley shuddered and pulled the bed covers over his head. 'Leave me alone – help,' he whimpered. The ghost blew the quilt from Riley's bed, lifted him up high in the air then headed for the window, laughing. Riley gave a pitiful cry as the ghost pulled him through the window. Where was his dream taking him?

Riley was whisked away to witness – once again – the chimney sweep boy.

Riley blinked and opened his eyes apprehensively. He scanned the room. He remembered the same large fireplace, but the picture of the man in black had gone. 'Remember this room?' growled the ghost. 'A young boy died in this chimney – I think you know who was responsible for that. Guess who has to clean our chimney in the manor now?'

'I guess it could be the terrible man with the needle stick who killed the boy. Do I have to clean the chimney now?' quizzed Riley.

The ghost laughed. 'You'll soon find out. Have a closer look.' In a gust of cold air, Riley headed towards the fireplace.

'But, but – I hated the chimney man,' pleaded Riley.

'Yes, perhaps,' laughed the ghost. 'But, you can still have a peep up the chimney.'

Riley slid and slithered up the chimney, his feet

dangling in the fireplace. Then a voice spoke from the chimney. 'Bullies, beware, or I'll give you a scare.' Then the room vanished.

'Glad to see yer back, Riley. Yer didn't get very far?'

Riley opened his eyes. 'Oh, no,' he sobbed. 'I'm back in the reformatory.'

'What's up, Riley?' asked the same voice. 'Going daft like old Bones along there?'

Riley shivered, seeing the rows of beds, then the terribly thin boys lying in them.

'They look like they're starving,' said Riley

'We're all like skeletons in 'ere, Riley – except you. So yer better watch out for Belter and Starver, 'cause they may wanna eat yer.'

A shadow appeared in the doorway. It was Belter. He wandered menacingly past each bed then stopped, glaring at the boy next to Riley.

'You must have helped this one escape,' he grunted. 'And now he's back, yer both planning sumfink. I'm gonna give yer a good beating.'

Belter whisked the cane from his side, held it in the air and gathered all his strength to strike. Riley didn't hesitate. He called out, 'Stop! Bully!' He dashed at the man's legs and knocked him off balance.

Riley tried to crawl away, but Belter had hold of his legs.

'What do we 'ave 'ere, then?' he asked cunningly. Riley went to stand up but Belter dragged him back down. 'See that floor?' Belter added. 'I'm gonna bury you under it.'

'Help me, someone,' pleaded Riley. He saw Daniel, Sophie and Tyler running towards him with Chip. The little dog sank his teeth into Belter's leg. All the boys gasped in disbelief. Belter shook Chip off, sending him flying through the air, landing on a startled boy's bed. There was a loud screech. The boys peeped over the tops of their blankets. Two ghosts swooped down from the rafters, flashing past all the beds, heading towards Belter like vengeful demons. They lifted him up and carried him off. Riley and all the boys watched, amazed, as Belter vanished into the night air. The room was silent, then they gave a cheer. But the cheering soon stopped when one ghost reappeared.

The ghost drifted towards Riley. 'Come with me, Master Riley,' he commanded. 'You do have some good in you – come and see more.'

One boy stood up. 'You're not daft, Riley! Tell 'em to take Starver as well. Don't forget to come back.'

The ghost took Riley to the same cotton mill. There he saw the faces of those he had bullied, including Daniel, Sophie and Tyler.

The ghost towered above everyone. 'You once visited the children here,' his voice boomed, sending a powerful gust of wind into Riley's face. 'You watched them suffer and mocked them.'

Riley's hair flew back.

The ghost thrust his long finger into Riley's face.

'Your other test is here.'

Riley flinched. He recognised the same shabby

176

children from his dream, and the same old machinery. Riley began to speak, but the ghost had disappeared.

'Put your backs into it!' demanded a man's voice. 'Supper's not till nine.' Riley glanced at a nasty-looking old man dressed like a scarecrow, in a scruffy black suit. He hunched over a long stick. Suddenly, the old man swivelled round, glaring with his bloodshot eyes. 'That means you as well, Riley,' he snarled, lifting the stick and cracking it down on a table. Riley jumped and scurried behind a machine, out of sight, as the room erupted into frenzied, activity.

'Come on, you scallywags,' shouted the man, his voice exploding along with the noisy rattling and banging of machinery.

Riley peered through a gap in the machine, watching the man striding towards him, waving his stick. He darted behind another machine then crouched next to a girl. 'Shush,' Riley whispered, holding his finger to his lips. But, the girl only smiled, touching her ears, indicating she was deaf.

The crafty old man was still looking for Riley. He crept along, prowling between the looms, glancing around all the time. Riley ducked out of sight. The man ran back and forth, trying to find him. Riley kept scampering away from his searching eyes, hiding behind children, all of whom seemed to be injured – with missing hands or fingers and deep gashes in their legs. He stared at their dull eyes and drawn cheeks as he crept nervously among them.

The vibrations of the spinning wheels rumbled

through the floor. The clonking of metal grew louder. Riley wiped the sweat from his face as he kept up the frightening game of hide and seek. Suddenly he tripped and lost sight of the wicked man. His eyes searched everywhere to find him. Then, to his horror, a pair of bloodshot eyes glared at him through a small gap in the machinery.

'Oh no, he's spotted me,' said Riley, frantically turning to face a nearby girl. 'Where can I go?'

The girl grabbed his arm and pointed to a door. But, in showing Riley the way out, her clothing caught in the wide rollers. She was pulled towards a cutting blade. Riley flinched, seeing the desperate face of the girl. He couldn't leave her now! Instinctively, he grabbed the girl's sleeve and held on to it, forcing the machine to slow.

'Got yer,' the man snapped, clutching Riley's collar.

'Get off me!' Riley snapped. 'I can't let go, she'll die!'

The man didn't budge. Neither did Riley. Eventually the machine creaked to a halt.

Riley grappled with the man and called for help. He saw Daniel, Sophie and Tyler running to help him. They jumped on the man and began hitting him. Riley couldn't believe his eyes as he crawled away from danger.

Riley noticed boys and girls crouching at the ends of the aisles. He lifted the girl from the machine and carried her to safety, comforting her. The din of the machines slowed, then stopped. A faint screeching whistled through the air; a surging wind howled through the roof trusses.

Two ghosts hovering above them with bright green eyes descended, grabbed the wicked man and carried him off up into the rafters. The light faded and the room fell into darkness.

Riley opened his eyes apprehensively then sighed with relief. 'This is my house.'

The ghost forced a grin at Riley. 'And who is this?'

'My little brother – but why do you want him?' asked Riley. The ghost gave a hideous laugh then disappeared.

'Where do you think we are now?' asked the ghost.

'School,' answered Riley.

'Then come with me, Billy Riley.'

They walked, listening to comments made by other boys and girls.

'Riley's a bully.'

'We don't like Riley – he's a coward.'

'I think the Geeks just hang around with Riley because they feel sorry for him.'

'I don't know why Riley is messed up – he's got a problem.'

'Do you think he will change?'

'He's heading for big trouble if he doesn't.'

Riley looked sheepishly up to the ghost. 'What kind of trouble?'

The ghost didn't answer. He touched Riley's hand and they vanished.

It was dark. Riley stretched out his hands, trying to feel something. 'I can't see. Where am I?' he asked.

'In your future – unless you want to go back to the chimney,' laughed the hideous ghost, appearing at his side.

'No, please,' begged Riley.

'Okay,' cackled the ghost.

Lights flickered, revealing a long room with rows of cells on each side.

'Take a look,' said the ghost. 'This is seven years from now.'

Riley stared into a prison cell at two mean-looking men. One was slim, with blond hair and a ponytail. The other was taller, heavily built with cropped dark hair. He had a long scar on his cheek.

'Who are they?' asked Riley.

The scarred man rushed to the bars of the cell. 'Let me out of 'ere!' he raged.

The blond man turned to face them. 'Keep calm, Billy Riley. You ain't gonna help your kid brother like that.'

'I've gotta help him – he's only thirteen and he's in trouble.'

Riley looked at the big ghost. 'Is that me in the future? What does he mean?'

The ghost laughed, and the bars of the cells shook. The two men ran backwards.

'There it goes again,' said the blond man. 'You're the cause of this, Billy. Ghosts will always follow you around.' The agitated Billy began pacing the floor.

Riley asked, 'Is that me in the cell in seven years' time? Please tell me what's going on. What's going to happen to my little brother in seven years?'

'Don't you care what's going to happen to you?' asked the ghost.

'Of course I do,' replied Riley.

'You will see soon.'

The light slowly faded, and they disappeared once again.

Riley had to find out more. 'I'm not going to be a murderer, am I?'

The ghost didn't answer so Riley spoke again. 'I know I've been a bully and done some bad things. Please, I don't want them to bully my brother Paul. Let me go home.'

The ghost took Riley's hand. The moon shone brightly. The ghost pointed across to a stone clad church lit up by floodlights. 'This is the path that could be your future, Billy Riley,' he said. They flew into the grounds of the church. Small lights shone up from the ground, illuminating the graveyard and casting shadows all around. The ghost led Riley by the hand as they went across the grass, past gravestones, and stopped at a marble headstone. Riley shivered as a chill wind wafted around the graves. The ghost thrust a ray of light at the stone and it glistened. Riley's eyes filled with tears as he silently read the words:

*Paul Riley, aged 14,*
*A boy who found peace.*
*Fond memories from a*
*Loving mum and brother Billy.*

'Impossible! My brother can't be dead!' cried Riley. The ghost spoke in a low voice. 'Your brother was bullied and tormented.'

He took Riley's hand and they drifted over to another gravestone. The ghost pointed again and the words lit up:

*Here lies Billy Riley, aged 21.*
*May he rest in peace.*

Riley immediately cried out, 'No, please! I don't want us to die.'

The ghost floated away into the cold night air, and Riley stood alone. 'Come back,' he whispered. 'Please take me home. I will change. Please.'

Riley sat up crying.

His mum rushed into his bedroom. 'It's okay, Billy, you're at home. You're safe. Did you have another nightmare? That's odd – Paul's just had a nightmare as well. His was about being bullied at school. If he is being bullied, that's terrible. I'm going to talk to the school. Promise you'll tell me if anything is wrong.'

'No, Mum – I mean, yes, Mum. Don't worry, Mum, nothing is going to happen. I'm going to change.'

The mystified Mrs Riley scratched her head.

Riley went to school that morning thinking. *That dream last night was horrible. I was in the reformatory and up a chimney where the boy died. The ghost frightened me to death. Oh no! I did die! Paul died too! Well, that's not going to happen. I'm gonna make sure it don't happen.*

# Chapter 20

Daniel, Sophie and Tyler stood in the playground of Middleton High, chatting.

Sophie shuddered. 'I talked to my mum and dad last night. I asked them if the school could be haunted. They laughed and said they didn't think so. I told them about the plaque on the wall shining. About Riley's eyes turning red and the things about my dream. Oh! And I said there's a written prophecy from the past. I said we had connected this to our school and the old manor and orphanage. They did listen, only I don't think they took me seriously, especially when I told them the prophecy came from *your* book. We need more help, Daniel. Riley has to stop bullying. He knows what you can do to him.'

'He should know,' replied Daniel. 'I think the wizard ghost is helping us and ghost Punishers only go after bullies.'

'I don't want to know,' interrupted Tyler. 'I just hope those creepy things don't come for me.'

'They won't, Tyler – anyway, it's our war against bullies now. With Buddy Wizard's help, we are going to get our own back.'

Nearby, a group of four older girls were bullying another girl.

'Girls bully just as much,' said Sophie. 'Look at that! We must stop them. You could help, Daniel.'

'Okay I'll try. Let's move a bit closer.'

'You're a spotty wimp,' remarked one girl, cruelly.

'You need to stop eating,' said another. The girls mocked their victim until one girl noticed they were being watched.

'You three jerks can get lost.'

'Who are you calling a jerk?' objected Tyler.

'You, beanpole.'

'You were told to go,' said another girl, pointing to Sophie. 'That means you as well, Spooky Brady.'

'Shove off,' Sophie replied. Daniel went to grip his chain but realised Mr North had it. But to his surprise a boy appeared. It was someone Daniel recognised, and he wore a tatty school uniform.

'It's Buddy Wizard,' Daniel whispered.

One of the girls scoffed at Buddy. 'Get back in your bin, scruffy.'

Buddy Wizard just smiled.

'We said get lost, freak.'

Buddy raised his eyebrows in contempt and moved closer to the girl who was being bullied.

'No, I'm here to stay,' replied Buddy Wizard. The bullies looked at each other and laughed.

'Who are you anyway, dirt boy?' one girl asked.

'Your worst nightmare,' replied Buddy. 'Here, look – my little pets don't like bullies either.' He opened up his hand to reveal several small white balls. The balls seemed hollow: something inside them stirred. Buddy

Wizard rolled them back and forth then blew them at the girls. The tiny white balls travelled towards them. The balls spun through the air, landing on each girl's cheek. Out crawled a hairy spider. The little spiders ran up the girls' faces, nestling into their hair. They touched their faces, trying to flick off the spiders.

'What was that?'

'You've got a red mark on your cheek,' said one girl.

'So have you.'

One girl froze until she managed to speak. 'He sent – SPIDERS!' She feverishly pulled at her hair then ran.

The girls panicked, screaming, staring at more balls coming towards them, this time with spiders crouching on top. The little creatures sat motionless, nearing the girls. Then, springing up, they revealed their nasty humped backs and tiny red eyes. One by one, they jumped onto the girls, who ran screaming across the playground, flapping their hands and shaking their hair, trying to knock off the spiders. Pupils laughed, bewildered, as the girls ran in all directions, panicking.

The girl standing next to Buddy Wizard smiled when Buddy Wizard whispered in her ear. 'That was a good lesson for those bullies.'

He walked away, leaving the mystified girl beaming.

In the meantime other troublemakers had arrived. They dawdled alongside Daniel, Sophie and Tyler.

'What are you creeps up to now?' one boy asked.

'Don't you lot realise that ghosts don't exist?' said another. They prowled menacingly around Daniel.

Billy Riley stood nearby, waiting to talk to Daniel.

'Why don't you lot leave them alone?' Riley remarked.

Miss Tubble charged through the kids in the playground. 'Break it up,' she bawled. 'What's going on here?'

Sophie didn't hesitate to answer. 'Those boys are picking on us, Miss.'

'We were only messing about,' said one boy.

'It didn't look like messing about to me,' Miss Tubble replied, frowning and shooing them away. 'You kids had better watch out, or you'll be on report.'

Later that morning, in the playground, Daniel wondered why Riley had stuck up for him. What could he be up to? But Sophie and Tyler had anticipated more trouble from the older kids, and Sophie remained vigilant.

'Here they come again,' she said. 'What shall we do?'

Daniel stepped forward, feeling for his chain again. 'I know what to do – leave this to me,' he said confidently, but he didn't have his chain. It was too late. The older boys were upon him.

'You're Brady, the magic kid, aren't you?'

Suddenly, a voice called out. 'Push off, you lot!'

It was Billy Riley!

'I told Mr North the truth about the chain. I'm sorry, Daniel – here it is.' Riley tossed the shiny bundle to Daniel, but to Daniel's horror an older boy snatched it from the air before he could reach it.

'What's this, then?' he asked, smirking.

'Give it back,' insisted Daniel, angrily. 'It's mine!'

The boys laughed teasingly, passing the chain around. Daniel held out his hand. 'Please, it's a present from someone special.'

One boy smirked then asked, 'Who?'

Riley butted in. 'You'll find out soon enough.'

'Let's think,' said the boy. 'I could sell it back to you. How much money have you got between you?'

'None,' said Daniel defiantly. 'We're not giving you a penny.'

The boy dangled the chain in front of Daniel's face.

'Tough guy, hey?' he said.

Daniel fixed his eyes on the swinging chain. So did the boy. The chain swung from side to side, left then right, again and again, mesmerising them both. They saw the hands and fingers of the chain moving, as though they were crawling. Each hand crept slowly to the next. The hands crept past each other, over and under, until they changed into a writhing snake – a tiny black snake with glistening black eyes began crawling over the boy's finger. The snake wrapped itself around the boy's finger, hissing.

The boy screamed. 'Quick! Get it off.' He threw the chain to the ground then jumped back, shaking his hand wildly in the air. 'Get it off! Get it off!' But the other boys couldn't see anything wrong.

'What's up?' one asked.

'What's the matter?' said the other.

'A snake!' he yelled, backing away. 'A snake – get it off me!'

Sophie smiled in amazement at Daniel. 'How did

your chain turn into a snake? I didn't see one. What happened?'

Tyler took off his glasses and blinked. 'I didn't see a snake either.'

'I did it with the chain, I think. I'm not sure how, but I was really angry.' Daniel picked up his chain. 'Anyway that'll teach him. That reminds me, where did Riley go?'

They looked around the playground, but he was nowhere to be seen.


The canteen was buzzing at lunchtime, with the usual clattering of plates and cutlery. The voices of children added to the din.

'Riley's over there,' Tyler remarked.

'Leave him to stew,' replied Daniel. 'He's learning. I don't think he'll trouble us for a while.' There was a sudden crash.

'Some boy just got tripped up,' said Sophie. A frail boy sprawled on the floor with his tray, plate and food scattered in front of him.

'Who tripped him up?' asked Daniel.

Sophie blamed a boy with blond hair. 'He did – and he meant to. Now his mates are having a good laugh.'

Daniel held his chain, looking fiercely at the blond boy. He held his chain tighter, willing it to work – for the blond boy to be punished. Then the blond boy's plate began to wobble. It rose up, hovered, then slammed straight into the boy's face, leaving a trail of bananas and custard spread all over him.

'I did it,' whispered Daniel, rapidly sitting back

down. Tyler and Sophie sat too, sniggering discreetly.

'Who threw that?' shouted the boy, wiping his face and looking at his mates. Within seconds an argument had erupted. At that moment, one end of their table lifted and all the plates and cutlery began to slide. The boys tried to grab their dinners but unfortunately they were too slow. The table shook, and the boys watched in horror as, one by one, their meals smashed onto the canteen floor. Then the table legs dropped back to the floor. The cutlery fell onto the pile of broken plates. As the last fork fell, the canteen fell silent.

All eyes focused on Miss Griffin and Miss Tubble charging along the aisle towards the messy scene. They glared at the heap of smashed plates and food, peering angrily at the confused boys.

Miss Griffin didn't hesitate. 'You lot are on report! On report, all of you.'

In the meantime, Miss Tubble attended to the tripped boy who could now stand, supported by Billy Riley.

'What happened to you?' she asked.

'He was tripped up, Miss,' replied Billy Riley. 'I'm helping him.'

Miss Tubble looked around at the other pupils then back to Billy Riley. 'I knew you had it in you – that's the spirit.'

Billy Riley answered humbly. 'I know, Miss, I've dreamed all about how you get to meet the spirit.'

Miss Tubble waddled away, pondering over Riley's words.

Daniel, Sophie and Tyler sat quietly, watching.

'How did you do that?' Sophie asked.

'I'm not sure,' replied Daniel. 'But they got a taste of their own medicine.'

Tyler laughed. 'Yeah, a taste of custard.'

'There are bullies everywhere,' Daniel said. 'They're right under our noses – and they're sneaky.'

# Chapter 21

Cold weather swept across the city, and in the days ahead Daniel had his wits about him yet he remained apprehensive. Anything – good or bad – could happen. He expected trouble and was prepared for the worst.

'Looks like I've stirred up a hornet's nest, Chip. Some of the other kids have been looking a bit threatening. I've heard them talking about me. We'll have to watch out. I'll tell Sophie and Tyler not to provoke trouble. We'll be ready for them, though.'

Chip wagged his tail then shuffled across the bed, snuggling up to Daniel.

'I need to tell Buddy Wizard that things are getting worse.'

At school, one of Daniel's favourite lessons was art and craft. The pupils were free to choose what they did. Some kids made pottery, others sewed, a few painted pictures, and one or two were looking for trouble. It wasn't long before the troublemakers seized their opportunity.

Two girls were painting a winter scene, a large painting that would eventually be displayed in the reception area of the school. The masterpiece was nearing completion and they often stood back admiring their work.

'You two are good at painting,' said one boy. 'Could you give us some advice?' The two girls readily obliged and went with the boy.

In the meantime, the boy's friends sneaked in and pounced. They blotched the painting, smearing black and red streaks over it, then crept off, laughing.

When they returned, the girls were devastated to see the smudges on their painting. They knew someone in the class must have done it. They were just heading to the teacher when Daniel intervened.

'The culprits are over there,' he said, trying to console the girls.

The bullies denied it. 'Push off, Brady, we didn't do anything. You must have smudged it.'

Daniel held onto his chain and concentrated for a few seconds. 'You two,' Daniel insisted, 'are going to clear the blotches from the trees and cover up the streaks you made in the snow.'

'Oh yeah? Make us,' one boy replied smugly.

Daniel concentrated harder, gripping his chain. 'Okay, I'll try.' Angrily, he thrust his finger at the black streaks on the picture – and magically they began to fade! At the same time, the two bullies began to shrink. They grew smaller and smaller until they finally disappeared. Daniel glanced at the floor, fearful, as two wisps of smoke rose back up in the air and trickled into the snow painting.

'Look!' said Daniel. 'There they are – little matchstick boys.'

The two girls glared into the painting, speechless.

They didn't move, apart from their eyes, which followed the movement across the scene. The two bullies ran across the snow in the picture. Back and forth they went, looking petrified, until one boy pointed out of the picture at Daniel.

'They can see us,' said Daniel. 'We must look like giants.'

The girls nodded in agreement, still in shock.

'Quick! Give me a clean paintbrush,' requested Daniel. A trembling hand passed a brush. Daniel dipped it into water then flicked the brush at the boys in the painting. 'I bet it's wet and cold there now,' Daniel said, laughing. 'Sorry.'

The two matchstick boys covered their heads as water splashed around them. Daniel then blew on the painting, causing swirling snow to fall on top of the boys. He moved his face closer to the painting, whispering, 'Clean the marks from the trees and cover up the rest of those black marks in the snow, or else.'

The two boys looked at each other, then at Daniel, before starting to do as he had asked. No one else in the classroom had seen anything, except the two spellbound girls.

'Giving your expert opinion, are we, Brady?' asked the art teacher, walking up to them. Daniel nodded then turned away, waiting for the teacher to go.

But something odd was happening to the painting.

'Did you paint a pack of wolves?' Daniel asked the girls. Mesmerised by the wolves that had now come alive in their painting, they nodded in shock. Daniel pointed at the picture. 'Paint a fire!'

The girls didn't hesitate. They painted the logs then the flames as Daniel watched. The fire suddenly came alive, flickering and making faint crackling noises. The tiny boys ran across the snow then huddled around the fire. The wolves cowered away, snarling.

Daniel wiped his forehead. 'For a minute I thought they might be goners.'

Meanwhile the activity in the classroom carried on as usual – even Sophie and Tyler didn't notice anything amiss. The girls continued to stare at their painting, dumbfounded. Daniel paced a few steps back and forth until he had an idea. He held his hand against the painting. He whispered, 'Come on you two, run onto my hand.' They climbed cautiously out of the picture, onto his hand, looking nervously behind them. Suddenly, a wolf jumped out of the picture. The boys turned in horror and ran across Daniel's hand, disappearing up his sleeve. Daniel gasped. The wolf was ready to pounce. He flicked his finger and sent the wolf reeling back into the picture.

'You've done a grand job, you girls,' said the art teacher, looking at the painting.

'Yes, sir,' said Daniel, jittery. 'It is.'

He felt a wriggling inside his sleeve.

The art teacher moved closer. 'It *almost* looks real.' He scratched his head, adjusted his glasses, and laughed. 'I thought I just saw something move.'

Daniel stepped in front of him and pointed over his shoulder. 'Please, sir, what do you think of my painting?'

The art teacher turned round. At that moment one of the boys crawled out of Daniel's sleeve and stood up on Daniel's hand alongside the teacher's ear. Daniel grabbed the boy and hid him in his jacket pocket. He then tried desperately to retrieve the other boy from his sleeve.

'I'll have a look at your masterpiece when it's finished,' the art teacher said, turning to look at Daniel. 'What is the problem with your arm, Daniel?'

Daniel shook the other boy down his sleeve and held him in his hand. 'Nothing.' Daniel held each boy in his hands, their tiny heads just visible.

'Here's a tip,' suggested the art teacher, looking back at Daniel's painting. 'You need to bring your painting more to life. A little more mind's eye is needed. Look into your imagination. Think of something unusual then try to paint that.'

'Yes, sir,' replied Daniel, feeling the boys wriggle in his hands. 'I'm learning how to make paintings come alive.'

'That's the spirit,' replied the art teacher, walking away. 'Keep trying, Daniel.'

Daniel opened his hands. 'I need you two to come back to life-size – please.' He placed the boys on top of a desk, gripped his chain then watched as they vanished. Oh no, he thought. They've gone. He inspected the desk and the floor, but there was no sign of them. He stared hopelessly around. 'I don't know what to do.' He then looked over at the two girls, who were whispering to each other, a bit shaky and confused, but continuing with their painting.

The teacher scrutinised the scene more closely, especially the log fire and the pack of wolves. He touched the little figures.

'Sorry, sorry,' he said to the girls. 'They seemed so real. I thought—'

Suddenly a few pupils tried to attract his attention. He scanned the room. 'You two sitting up there – get down this instant!'

Everyone looked up at two boys perched high in an alcove.

'That'll teach them to bully,' said Daniel. Sophie and Tyler immediately smiled at Daniel, wondering if he had somehow had anything to do with the boys.

Later that day the three strolled to the Christmas play rehearsals.

'You wouldn't believe what just happened in art,' Daniel said.

Tyler nodded his head. 'Oh yes, we would – wouldn't we, Sophie?'

'I'm not sure if this play is a good idea,' complained Sophie. 'We're not very popular.'

'It's got nothing to do with the play,' said Daniel, reassuringly. 'We're exposing the bullies and they don't like it.'

'What happens if we expose scores of bullies?' asked Sophie. 'They'll come after us.'

'I'll protect you,' said Daniel.

Tyler took off his ghost hood. 'How can you protect us?'

'I'll tell Buddy Wizard. He'll protect you.'

Miss White interrupted. 'Get ready, ghosts.'

The three adjusted their outfits then walked up onto the stage to the sound of ghostly music. They crept eerily around to the side of the painted gates where the gatekeeper kept guard.

'Riley's the new gatekeeper,' whispered Daniel. 'Spread out. He's only supposed to get a glimpse of us before we go through the wall.'

Riley acted the part well. He was on guard, looking left then right. He drew his sword. The ghosts quickly made their exit through a compartment in the wall then ducked undetected, behind Riley. The audience would be able to see the ghosts through the bars. The ghosts moved back and forth or sideways, hiding, whenever Riley tried to look for them.

They weren't in the next scene. Daniel decided this was a good time to speak to him. 'Billy Riley, thanks for sticking up for me. I hope it's not a ploy of yours, because it won't work. Do you understand?'

Riley nodded.

'We've got more problems with bullies. They're all after us now. Don't expect any sympathy if they come after you.'

'Okay,' Riley whispered.

Daniel turned his attention to Sophie and Tyler. 'He had better watch out.'

'We know,' said Sophie.

# Chapter 22

The following day Daniel was back at school, walking along the north wing corridor, captivated by the medieval-looking lights, unaware that a teacher stood in his path.

'Good morning, Daniel,' said Miss White. 'Fascinating, aren't they?'

'Sorry, Miss. Er, what?'

'They say that the lights are similar to those that hung from this very spot hundreds of years ago. When the school was built they thought it a good idea to try and replicate some of the manor's lamps here.'

Daniel gulped. 'Did they?'

Miss White smiled. 'There are rumours about the school being haunted, but I don't think that's true.'

Daniel, reluctant to discuss any more, began to edge away thinking she might not believe him. 'I've g-got to go to maths. Sorry, Miss.'

Daniel sat listening in Miss Tubble's maths lesson.

'Quiet now,' she said glaring around the classroom. 'Today's lesson is all about speed and distance.'

Sophie whispered to Daniel. 'Are we safe now?'

Miss Tubble overheard the whispering. 'You're very talkative, Sophie Little. Are you excited about the school play tonight?'

She strolled towards Sophie. 'Well, answer this. How fast would a ghost need to travel to catch the speed of sound?'

Sophie bowed her head. 'Um, sorry, Miss, I don't know.'

Miss Tubble's eyes flashed to Daniel. 'Do you know, Brady?'

'About seven hundred and sixty miles per hour, Miss.'

Miss Tubble gave a little clap. 'Well done, Daniel. No one would catch you then, would they?'

Daniel raised his eyebrows. 'N-no, Miss.'

Tyler leaned closer to Daniel. 'I wonder if she knows about the prophecy?' Miss Tubble tutted at Tyler then walked to the whiteboard, wrote a few numbers, then snapped the lid back on her pen.

'I hope she's not a witch,' said Sophie.

After the lesson, Daniel was out in the playground with Tyler and Sophie. As he had expected, trouble was close by.

'Watch where you're going, Brady,' said a girl, pushing past. Sophie glared daggers at the girl.

'Forget her, Sophie,' said Daniel calmly. 'She's just another bully. I told you we were in for it. Don't worry. Buddy Wizard will protect us from bullies.'

Suddenly Tyler shouted, 'Look out!'

Daniel immediately thrust out his hand and caught a stone that had been thrown at him.

'Who threw that?' asked Sophie.

Tyler replied, 'Don't know, but Riley's running towards the school.'

A strange screeching noise came from overhead, and Daniel looked hesitantly up to the sky. 'I've heard that sound before in my bedroom.'

The faint image of a man's face gradually appeared in the sky.

Several children noticed it too.

The face in the sky grew brighter. Large, bloodshot eyes peered at them. 'Oh, I can see it now,' Sophie said.

Tyler also looked up, stepping backwards, and bumped into a taller boy. 'Sorry,' he said.

'Look where you're going, jerk.'

Another boy laughed. 'He's a creep. He hangs around with magic boy Brady.'

The boys turned on Daniel, pushing him back and forth, unaware that a ghostly figure looked down, judging them. They continued to laugh at Daniel and mock him, until an almighty surge of wind blew over their heads. It lifted the two boys off their feet. They flew through the air and landed in a heap.

'What's going on, Daniel?' asked Mr Shaw, fighting the swirling wind.

'Look, sir – there's a strange image in the sky, like a face. The strong wind blew over those two muppets – I mean, boys.'

Everyone struggled to stand upright as the wind roared about them.

Mr Shaw kept straining his eyes and recognised a shadowy figure.

'Sophie thought it was some sort of ghost,' remarked Daniel.

'Do you mean you two actually established it was a ghost?'

'Yes, sir.'

Mr Shaw glanced up again then leaned towards Tyler for some answers. 'I can't see anything now. Can you see anything, Tyler?'

The wind whistled and Tyler shouted, 'Er, yes and no, sir.'

Mr Shaw switched his attention to Sophie, cupping his hands to shout. 'Daniel said you saw a ghost, and who's Buddy Wizard?'

Sophie wavered in the strong wind. 'Yes, I did see something, sir. Only … it's best if you ask Daniel about Buddy Wizard.'

Daniel remained apprehensive about revealing the truth about Buddy Wizard. He didn't know whether or not Mr Shaw would believe him. 'He's just someone I see in my dreams, sir. I read about Middleton Manor and the old orphanage. I'm fascinated by its history.'

Gradually the wind stopped blowing. Everything seemed calm.

'The old castle and manor are not to be taken lightly, Daniel,' said Mr Shaw, lowering his voice. 'Right. The strange wind has stopped. I'll need to discuss this with the other teachers. I must go. I'll see you lot at tonight's performance.' Mr Shaw went away, glancing back, suspicious of Daniel, wondering if he could be involved with the unusual happenings in the school.

At lunchtime, the staffroom was busier than usual.

'I believe there's a connection,' Mr Shaw remarked. 'The children have reported sightings at the school. The wind blew furiously in the playground today. It then suddenly stopped. We cannot deny that this *could* be the beginning of the prophecy.'

Several teachers nodded in agreement.

'A number of pupils have claimed that Daniel Brady had some sort of power. We have checked his ancestors as far as possible.'

Miss White continued. 'We are quite certain that some of the pupils have seen something. If so, these occurrences must be connected. The history of the old orphanage is documented in the library. There are rumours that the school is haunted. Our school could be connected to this prophecy.'

Mr North spoke. 'Brady's silver chain was burning hot.'

Miss Griffin butted in. 'I always suspected Brady could have something up his sleeve.'

The art teacher scratched his head. 'Yes, come to think of it, so did I.'

'Strange things have definitely been taking place,' added Miss Tubble.

'Well, all I can suggest is that we keep a close eye out,' said Mr Shaw.

Later that day, Daniel, Sophie and Tyler left their geography lesson, discussing ghosts. Four older girls stood outside menacingly, blocking the corridor.

'Oh no, here we go again,' said Daniel. 'I overheard

some girls saying that we're all weird. They said I'm doing magic. That's not good, Sophie. Is it Tyler?'

'Yeah right, tell 'em to butt out.'

Sophie smiled. 'I've seen Riley hanging around with those girls. He could have spoken to them about you. I am dying to see this.' She laughed. 'I heard them say we're in for it.'

'Don't you mean *they're* in for it?' replied Daniel, pointing to four creepy faces that were appearing above the girls' heads. 'It's the Punishers! They're in the school!'

They waited, watching and listening, a few metres away. The girls joked, gesturing towards Sophie, unaware of what lurked above them.

'We want to see if your boyfriend is really magic, little girl.'

'Yeah, could you ask him to give us some dosh?'

'Ha,' replied Sophie. 'I suggest you ask him – but don't look up.'

Just then, a blob of slime dropped onto one girl's head and slithered down her forehead. She wiped the slime away with her fingers; inspected it then glared up. She shuddered then let out a scream. The other girls looked at her, confused, then at the ceiling. They didn't hang around. They all dashed along the corridor, screaming.

Soon, teachers were on the scene.

Then Mr North, the headmaster, arrived. 'What's going on, Mr Shaw?' he asked.

'I don't know. We've had these strange occurrences before, but this time it's different.'

Mr North faltered. 'You mean the prophecy?'

'I don't know,' replied Mr Shaw.

'Leave this to me,' interrupted Miss Griffin. 'I'll deal with it.'

She marched smartly up to the crowd of staring pupils. 'There's nothing to see here. Off you go to class. Anyone would think you had seen a ghost!'

'I think we did see one,' blurted a Year 10 boy. 'My mates ran, miss.'

An older girl joined in. 'My friends ran too after I spotted one.'

With that, two whimpering girls fainted.

'That was really freaky,' said Sophie, 'especially for those four.'

'I'm not looking forward to the play,' sighed Tyler. 'Not after seeing ghosts. That's crazy. *We're* the ghosts tonight.'

'I'm glad we're not the bullies,' Daniel remarked. 'Let's get out of here.'

Later that day a sense of anticipation filled the school. The assembly hall began to fill up with parents and pupils. Teachers and older pupils helped the elderly to their seats, and excitement filled the faces of children, who fidgeted in their seats, eager to see the play.

# Chapter 23

There was a banner stretched across the hall entrance.

*THE GHOSTS OF MIDDLETON MANOR*

Daniel peeked through the curtain at the audience. 'There's my mum, dad and big-headed sister,' he said jovially.

Tyler also peered through the curtain. 'My mum, dad and older brother should be here.'

Sophie nudged her way in, lower down. 'There's my mum and dad.'

'Can I have a look?' asked a familiar voice. 'And I didn't throw that stone at you three.'

Daniel spun round to face Riley.

'Okay, I believe you, Billy,' he said, but Tyler and Sophie sneered.

'I know who did throw the stone, though,' said Riley.

'It doesn't matter,' replied Daniel. 'I know someone who will stop all the bullying going on here.'

'I know you do,' said Riley. 'I've learned a lesson.'

'We don't believe you,' said Sophie coldly.

'Off the stage, you four,' said Miss White, coming

up behind them. 'The curtain will be going up shortly.'

The lights dimmed and the buzz of voices gradually quietened. The orchestra started to play: a spooky, atmospheric piece. The curtains slowly parted. There was a clatter of thunder and streaks of lightning. On stage there was a house beyond a spooky forest. Three weary travellers sat at the foot of an old oak tree, discussing where they had come from and where they were heading.

'Ghosts, are you ready?' asked Miss White. 'Don't forget, the bang is loud and the lights will dazzle you.'

The ghosts crept up onto the stage, barely visible in the dark. Thunder sounded and lightning flashed. The stage was briefly illuminated, revealing the three scary ghosts disappearing behind a clump of plastic bushes next to the imitation oak tree. They crouched and hid, waiting.

'Wait for it,' whispered Daniel.

'I'm ready,' said Sophie.

'Me too, man.'

Another flash lit up the stage. Two ghosts sprang up, showing their white hooded cloaks. The audience gasped. However, Sophie, the third ghost, screamed and jumped backwards.

'That scream wasn't in the script,' said Mr Shaw, standing backstage.

Meanwhile, in the audience, Mrs Brady craned her neck to see over the people in front of her. 'We only saw two ghosts,' she said. 'Who's missing?'

Back on stage, Sophie sat down. She looked petrified.

'What's wrong, Sophie?' whispered Daniel, sitting

with her.

Sophie shuffled towards Daniel then responded. 'I saw a face on that tree.'

'What?'

Sophie pointed. 'There – on the trunk.'

'Whoa, man, there can't be,' whispered Tyler apprehensively. All three sat behind the tree. They searched in vain for a face – until Tyler had an idea. He felt for the face. He carefully ran his hand over the rough surface. Suddenly, a flash lit up the stage. His eyes nearly popped out of his head.

Tyler screamed, diving backwards. Daniel and Sophie jumped too.

'That's not in the script either,' said Miss White, backstage.

Sophie covered her eyes then peeked through her fingers.

'We've got to get off stage,' she whispered.

Daniel examined the tree inquisitively, trying to distinguish a face. 'I don't think that is a face,' he said, unconvincingly. But as he spoke, a bright face lit up. It stretched out of the tree, followed by a neck then a small, stubby body with legs and arms. The tree-man stepped onto the stage. Daniel, Tyler and Sophie scrambled to their feet and ran across the stage, falling one by one through the trapdoor.

'Good effects,' said Mr Brady, glued to the action. 'Realistic screams too.'

'Yes, dear,' whispered Mrs Brady, 'now shush.'

Daniel, Tyler and Sophie lay on the floor, groaning,

before scrambling to their feet and emerging backstage. They were met by Miss Griffin.

'What's the matter with you three? Scared of the dark?'

'Yes, Miss,' said Sophie. 'The tree on stage is creepy.'

'It just looks creepy,' said Miss Griffin. 'It won't hurt you.'

'I told her that,' Daniel said. 'Only she wouldn't listen.'

Tyler agreed with Sophie. 'I wouldn't listen either.'

Most of the audience were captivated by the play but the odd critic, like Daniel's sister Emily, wasn't impressed.

'Stupid play,' she muttered. 'I thought it was supposed to be scary.'

'Shush,' said Mrs Brady. 'Someone will hear you.'

Emily stared coolly up at the high ceiling, uninterested in the play. Instead, she became mesmerised by the shadows drifting towards the stage. Her eyes tracked the shapes as they neared the stage. Then, to her amazement, one shadow turned and came back. *Am I dreaming?* she thought. *Or can I really see two shiny eyes peering down at me?* Emily looked away, then up again. *Oh no, something is looking down.* Each time she glanced up, the shadow had moved. It was staring at someone else. She kept rubbing her eyes until it disappeared.

'Mum, Dad…'

'What, Emily?' asked Mrs Brady.

'I think there's something on the ceiling. It was moving, and looking at me.'

'No! Where?' asked Mrs Brady, glancing up apprehensively. 'Surely not! What made you think that? I haven't seen anything.'

Backstage, boys and girls chatted, waiting for their cue.

'I think we should tell Mr Shaw about that tree,' suggested Sophie.

Daniel laughed. 'Sure! And by the way, sir, there's a live creepy tree sneaking around somewhere.'

'Who's creeping around, Brady?' asked Mr Shaw, standing close by.

Tyler stood up. 'We're not sure, sir, but, we think you should look at something on stage.'

'I knew you lot had a trick up your sleeve,' said Mr Shaw. 'Who else is involved?'

Sophie snapped back. 'It's nothing to do with me, sir.'

'Nor me, sir,' said Tyler.

Mr Shaw turned his attention to Daniel. 'So let's have a look on stage.'

The scene ended. The curtains closed. There was rapturous applause, and the stage hands ran on stage to change the scenery.

The three trailed Mr Shaw around on stage. 'I can't see anything unusual,' he said. 'What am I supposed to be looking for?'

The tree and bushes had been pushed to one side and the exterior of the manor house now occupied the stage, with the gatekeeper, Riley, standing guard at the foot of the imitation iron gates.

'Is Riley involved in any of this?' asked Mr Shaw, turning to look at Billy.

Sophie piped up. 'He was, sir.'

What do you mean, was?

Daniel interrupted, 'Well, sir, it's been going on for some time, but Riley may be cured.'

Mr Shaw seemed annoyed. 'What do you mean, cured? Cured of what, Daniel Brady?'

'Cured of bullying.'

'What's bullying got to do with you lot planning to sabotage my play?'

'We're not going to sabotage your play! You asked us to be in it, didn't you? We wouldn't do that.'

'Did someone say we would?' snapped Tyler.

'Too many kids around here are lying, sir,' explained Daniel.

'Look, we haven't got time to discuss this now, Daniel. The play must go on.'

'Off the stage, everyone,' called Miss White. 'The next scene is about to begin.'


The Brady family sat watching as the play continued.

Mr Brady whispered. 'The sound and lighting effects are excellent. I wonder how they get the eerie sounds, though – listen.'

They heard the faint sound of distant voices. The audience looked rapt.

'Sounds like children chattering,' remarked Mrs Brady.

'They're probably ghosts,' said Emily. 'Considering

the school's reputation…'

'Get ready, ghosts,' prompted Miss Tubble, backstage. The three ghosts crept up the steps then dodged behind Riley, the gatekeeper, who waited in front of the iron gates, holding up a lantern. The curtains parted and the street scene came alive with actors and actresses, flocking on stage, celebrating and dancing. This allowed Daniel to speak to Billy Riley.

'Billy Riley,' Daniel whispered. 'Can you hear me?'

Riley nodded discreetly.

'There's a real ghost somewhere on stage, so be careful.'

Riley fidgeted then wiped his forehead.

Suddenly, the lights flickered.

'That's all we need,' remarked Miss Griffin. 'A power cut.' She noticed a trailing power supply cable near the storeroom. 'Is that cable safe? It's drooping over that miniature tree.'

'Shouldn't affect anything,' answered Mr Shaw. 'But I'll move it.' He was walking towards the tree when there was a flash. Electricity surged through the tree and lit up its branches. At that moment the lights all went out backstage, then a few flickered back on.

'Boy, that was lucky,' gasped Mr Shaw. 'I could have been electrocuted.'

'Stay still, boys and girls,' said Miss Tubble. 'There's nothing to worry about. It's just a power surge.' She flicked the switch and the other lights came back on. Miss Griffin glanced at the tree, and noticed something drifting away from it.

'Look!' she said, flinching. 'It's—'

'*A ghost!*' shrieked Mr Shaw. 'Stand back – they're here! Don't panic.' He signalled everyone to keep back. The ghostly image forming from the tree began to take the shape of a boy.

Miss Griffin covered her eyes. 'Don't let the children see this.'

Miss Tubble flapped her hands to shoo the children away. The lights flickered on and off.

'Quick! Where's Daniel Brady?' Mr Shaw asked. 'Get him in here – *now!*'

'I'll get him,' replied Miss Tubble, stumbling towards the little door under the stage.

'Okay, cordon the area off,' Mr Shaw added, pulling a partition across the floor. The children all gathered at the other end of the room, looking anxious, until the small stage door flew open and Miss Tubble crawled out, followed by Daniel.

A desperate Mr Shaw beckoned Daniel over. 'It's as we expected, Daniel. You're part of this prophecy. And it looks like your ancestors may have turned up.'

'What do you mean, *my* ancestors?'

Mr Shaw peeled back the edge of the screen. 'Take a look.'

Daniel peered through the gap then jumped back. 'He's no relation to me – he's a Punisher.' They must have entered the school through the plaque or the crossover link, he thought.

A small ghost whizzed past them and flew underneath the stage, chased by a larger, mean-looking ghost.

'I think I'm going to faint,' said Miss Griffin.

Mr Shaw wiped his forehead. 'What on earth is a Punisher, Daniel?'

'He's a nasty ghost, sir and he's chasing a good ghost.'

'I think I'm going to faint too,' said Miss Tubble, holding her forehead.

Meanwhile, the audience clapped enthusiastically at the fake ghosts. Sophie and Tyler peered through the bars behind Riley.

The audience shouted: 'Look! There's a ghost.'

On stage, the baron looked around and didn't see anything. He called back at the audience, 'Oh no, there isn't.'

Sophie the ghost appeared at the bars again.

The audience called out, 'Oh yes, there is.'

'Where?' asked the baron.

'Behind you,' heckled the audience.

The baron looked again – but this time a *real* giant ghost towered above him, sneering. Billy Riley gasped and began to edge backwards, shivering.

'Keep still, Billy,' said Sophie, standing behind the bars.

'Stay cool, man,' added Tyler, popping up next to Sophie. 'Daniel will sort this out.'

People in the audience gasped, along with Mrs Brady and Emily.

'Now that's what I call realistic,' said an excited Mr Brady. 'It must be a hologram.'

'Which one is Daniel?' asked Emily.

'I don't know,' replied Mrs Brady.

Emily pointed at the big ghost on stage. 'That's not Daniel.'

All eyes focused on the real ghost, who sneered scornfully at the audience. The nasty ghost leaned forward and blew. A gust of wind surged past the baron and into the audience.

'What terrific special effects,' said Mr Brady, feeling the wind on his face. 'How did they do that?'

Mrs Brady fidgeted. 'It's a bit scary for kids.'

Emily slid lower in her seat. 'It's getting *too* scary.'

Slowly, the curtains closed. Teachers encouraged the audience to applaud.

Backstage, Mr Shaw held on to Daniel's arm. 'I'm not letting you out of my sight until we find those two ghosts.'

A tall sixth-form girl immediately signalled Mr Shaw. 'Sir, sir, Miss White wants you on stage. She says it's urgent.'

Just then the lights flashed, and there were ominous groans.

Mr Shaw wanted an explanation from Daniel. 'What's going on, now, Brady?'

'The ghosts don't like bullies, sir. That's why they're appearing in the school. The ghosts may have come now because they must know who the bullies are. Perhaps they think bullies are in the play?'

The girls and boys all looked at each other and shuffled to one side, leaving one boy and a girl standing on their own.

Mr Shaw shook his head. 'I don't believe this. What's happening?'

Miss Tubble waddled towards him. 'It's okay,' she said, 'Everything is going to plan.' Seconds later the music sounded and the curtains parted for the last scene. The Brady family, and the rest of the audience, sat motionless with expectation. Backstage, the actors gathered for the spectacular ending of *The Ghosts of Middleton Manor.*

Mrs Brady gazed at the lovely lights on the ceiling. 'They look like they're moving,' she commented.

Emily looked up. 'They look like eyes, Mum, peering down.'

'More holograms, no doubt,' chuckled Mr Brady. 'It's all clever stuff, you know.'

Emily looked left then right. The shadows were turning into blue shapes.

'Mum,' she said. 'Look up. Are they *eyes?*'

Mr and Mrs Brady looked up, along with several other people in the audience…

'Oh my God,' said Mr Shaw. 'What's going on? Look!'

He squirmed with other members of staff, peering through the partly open curtain in the wings. A procession of ghosts moved along the ceiling at either side of the hall, looking down on the bewildered audience. One by one they stopped and hung motionless, as if guarding the hall. Heads turned. There were nervous giggles. Light-hearted comments filled the air. Everyone whispered, 'Holograms – they're holograms – that explains it.'

'Quick, start the performance,' said Mr Shaw. 'Sound the trumpets – clap.'

The staff clapped. It worked. The audience clapped along enthusiastically. The play continued, with most of the audience seeing the ghosts as a fascinating distraction.

'This school has always been creepy, Mum. I've heard about people seeing ghosts here – and some of those up there look real.'

'Shush, Emily, not now,' said Mrs Brady.

The play was in full swing. The wicked baron, having bullied everyone in the past, was set to pay for his sins in the haunted castle. The ghosts of Middleton Manor found him guilty, and the townsfolk were eager to witness his punishment. The cast gathered around the baron on stage. The three ghosts, Daniel, Sophie and Tyler, were on stage, standing behind Riley. The townsfolk booed and hissed at the baron, who cowered on the floor.

'Please save me,' he begged.

The mayor spoke loudly. 'Shall we punish the baron? All those in favour, shout aye, and all those against, shout nay.'

The audience erupted with a deafening 'Aye!'

Then there was a screeching noise from the back of the hall.

'I know that noise,' said Daniel.

Billy Riley did too. 'So do I,' he said, retreating and treading on Sophie's foot. She yelped.

The screeching continued. Two straggly-haired ghosts with wrinkled faces flew over the audience before swooping over the baron. They hovered menacingly around, their eyes intense, before flying across the stage to lift the baron up. Riley cringed as the ghosts took hold of the baron and then stared back at him. The other boys and girls on stage froze. Tyler and Sophie edged backwards. But Daniel gripped his chain. His fist glowed. A shining ball spun from his hand and swirled through the air, heading towards the ghosts. The ball hit one ghost. They dropped the baron and flew off over the audience, vanishing in a cloud of mist.

'Clap,' shouted Mr Shaw. 'Quickly, everyone clap.'

There were a few claps, then the audience began to clap louder. People stood to applaud. The clapping grew louder, until the hall filled with applause.

'Wow!' said Mr Brady, clapping enthusiastically.

'Where are the holograms?' replied Mrs Brady, looking around.

But all the ghosts had disappeared.

'It was spooky,' said Emily. 'That's what it was – spooky and really scary. It was all too realistic. I bet Daniel has something to do with this. I've overheard him talking about ghosts to his friends. We need to ask him why he's so secretive? I hope he's okay.'

# Chapter 24

The day began cold, and the atmosphere was also chilly at Middleton High, especially in the headmaster's office, where Mr North and Mr Shaw spoke to Daniel.

'That was a spectacular show you put on last night, Daniel,' said Mr North. 'I know you were involved.'

Daniel kept quiet, watching Mr North pace up and down in front of Mr Shaw.

'Before you try to explain,' said Mr Shaw, 'I must tell you that something serious has happened. Twenty boys and girls from this school have gone missing from their homes. They disappeared last night.'

*'What?'* said the shocked Daniel. 'That's got nothing to do with me, sir.'

Mr North frowned. 'From what we have heard, we do think it has something to do with you, Daniel. Their parents were all frantic this morning and the phones have been ringing non-stop. We have police searching everywhere. Reporters are asking all sorts of questions. Pupils here are worried. Everyone wants answers. The police want to question you and your friends.'

But, Daniel stopped listening. His eyes wandered out of the headmaster's window, and for a split second he thought he saw a reflection of a ghost. He took his eyes away from the window as Miss White walked into the office.

'Hello, Daniel,' said a flustered Miss White. 'It was a bit of a ghostly play last night, wasn't it?'

She handed Mr Shaw a note.

'Thank you for the information, Miss White. We'll sort this out now.' He placed his hands on the table, thought for a moment, before stating the facts to Daniel. 'For a few years now, there have been rumours that this school is haunted. There's an ancient prophecy that tells of a boy who will attend our school. This boy is a descendant of a revolting man who was responsible for the death of many people, including children, a few centuries ago at Middleton Manor and school orphanage. The prophecy goes on to say that this boy will bring ghosts here, and they will destroy anything or anyone that stands in their way.'

Daniel leaped out of his seat. 'That's not true. Buddy Wizard wouldn't lie to me.'

Mr North slapped his hand on the table. '*Who* is this Buddy Wizard we keep hearing about?'

'Calm down,' suggested Mr Shaw. 'I'm sure we'll find out soon enough.' He placed his hand on Daniel's shoulder. 'Look,' he said, reassuringly, 'I could only trace your family tree back a couple of hundred years, so we don't know for certain if you have any connection to the child in the prophecy.'

'I'm not certain either. Can I go now, sir?'

'Yes, Daniel, but remember ghosts were in action last night, so be careful.'

Mr Shaw slid his hand in his pocket and took out the shiny pendant. 'I may have dreamed about your ghost some time ago. I found this outside my front door. Mr North said the design was very similar to that of the chain. It has tiny hands, and could have some connection to you – so take it.'

Daniel immediately saw that the hands on the pendant looked like those on his chain. 'Thank you, sir. I'll take good care of it.'

'Okay, run along now, Brady,' said Mr North, opening the door. 'And watch your step.'

'Be careful, Daniel,' warned Mr Shaw. 'You don't know what you're dealing with. I will be speaking to your parents.'

Daniel hurried along the corridor, looking at the pendant. It had a link that would fit his chain. He hurried past two police officers, who were in school to interview students about the girls and boys who had disappeared the previous night. Students looked worried. They huddled in small groups, discussing what could have happened to their friends. A few girls were in tears. Some milled around, silent. The atmosphere was bleak. A few people pointed at Daniel, whispering his name. He tried to avoid everyone, but knew that was impossible. He felt under pressure.

Daniel ran home and turned the key in his front door.

'Chip, Chip, where are you?'

The little dog scurried through the hall, slid along the floor and leaped into Daniel's arms. Daniel gave him a big hug then carried him upstairs. They lay on the bed. Daniel told Chip what had happened.

'I'm in trouble now, Chip. I walked out of school because everyone kept talking about me. I couldn't stand it any longer.'

Daniel was sprawled on his bed, about to nod off to sleep, when he heard his mum's voice.

'What terrible news,' she said. 'How could all those children disappear? Where on earth could they be? Their parents must be worried sick. I just heard the news. They want anyone who has any information to call the police. Did you hear anything at school, Daniel? Were any of the kidnapped children at the play?'

Daniel leaped off the bed. 'I don't know, Mum!' He began thinking, *this is all my fault.*

At that moment, the front door bell rang. Mrs Brady hurried downstairs. Daniel clambered off the bed to listen to her, and find out who was at the door, but then something touched his shoulder.

'Buddy Wizard, you frightened me to death,' said the shocked Daniel.

'Sorry, Master Daniel, but we have to depart.'

'Depart where?'

'We need to rescue your school friends.'

'They're not my friends, and how can I rescue them?'

Mrs Brady had gone outside, but no one was there. She closed the door then began to walk up the stairs. 'Someone is playing a trick on me,' she said.

Buddy Wizard held out his hand. 'Make haste, Daniel – come.'

'No, I'm not going back there.'

The doorbell rang again.

'Not again!' said Mrs Brady.

She trudged down the stairs then opened the door, cursing. 'Oh, sorry,' she said, 'I thought you were—'

'Does Daniel Brady live here?' asked a burly police officer.

Mrs Brady was shocked. 'Yes, why? What has he done?'

'I just want to have a chat with him, about someone called Buddy Wizard.'

'Who?' asked Mrs Brady. She called out, 'Daniel!'

There was no reply.

***

The dark shadowy grey walls of Middleton Manor's long corridor stretched out in front of Daniel. It was 1760. His eyes followed the line of flickering candles that stretched along the dimly lit path. He knew what lay ahead, and shivered at the thought of once again meeting the Punishers.

Buddy Wizard beckoned Daniel. 'Come with me – and stay quiet. We must venture a different path.'

Daniel crept cautiously behind him. 'I think I should have stayed at home.'

'Shush.'

Daniel followed through the arched doorway and began to descend a sloping tunnel, glad to be away from the ghostly corridor yet fearful of going to the old castle's dungeons. Buddy Wizard glanced back at Daniel. 'No one will detect you here. Everyone is afraid of the swamps – even the Punishers. There are dangers by these waters.'

'Great. That's nice to know,' whispered Daniel.

Candles flickered as they proceeded cautiously, heading deeper and deeper underground. Daniel sensed the curved ceiling gradually lowering and felt the walls of the tunnel narrowing. The light faded so much that Daniel struggled to see the way ahead. He could only see the glowing figure of Buddy Wizard moving further away into the darkness.

'Wait for me,' Daniel called out. The tunnel echoed his words back to him.

Buddy Wizard paused. 'Shush.' The candles began to fade. It was becoming darker.

Daniel stretched his hands out in front of him, feeling the way forward. 'Wait for me,' he whispered. 'Please, Buddy.'

A circle of light floated through the air towards Daniel. 'Take hold of the light.'

Daniel reached out and caught a glowing staff. The light grew brighter. In his hand he now held a shining sceptre. 'Wow,' he said, thrilled.

'Behold the shining sceptre, Daniel, once the King's treasure. He gave this to my ancestors with his blessing. The sword passed to me and remained hidden, until now. Within you the light now appears; it is, as I expected.'

Daniel lit up the tunnel as it twisted and turned, catching glimpses of Buddy Wizard. He hesitated past dark shadows on damp walls, dodged past strange noises, stepped over eerie creatures, and nearly jumped out of his skin when a flurry of birds flew out of a hidden cave, narrowly missing him.

Daniel descended with Buddy into the darkness of the tunnel, heading towards a distant light. Am I near the old castle? he thought. He wanted to go faster. There was a rumble of thunder. A blast of air struck his face.

'Do not be concerned, Daniel,' said the reassuring Buddy Wizard. 'It is only the force of the swamp – she blows hot and cold.'

Daniel wiped his forehead and lowered the sceptre. To his astonishment, it transformed back into a shining sword.

Daniel swung the sword back and forth. 'Let me at them!'

Daylight lit up the entrance to the tunnel, revealing a multitude of weeds trailing around it. Daniel struck the brambles with his sword, eager to test it. He thrust it again and again, slicing the bushes and shrubbery.

They emerged out of the tunnel onto a narrow path. Daniel gazed up at the walls of the old castle towering above him. He could see the narrow path that ran alongside the stone wall. On one side ran a bubbling stream and the unwelcoming swamp. The sun shone low in the sky, casting a fiery red glow through nearby trees. Daniel strode along. Then the water erupted in a frenzy of action.

A ball of steam rose from the surface, exploding into a cascading fountain of water. Instinctively, Daniel ducked. He thrust his sword towards the swamp, ready to defend himself, but soon realised that this wasn't the time for acting.

'Hey, wait for me,' he called out, hurrying after Buddy Wizard. But his shout had attracted something else. A huge dragon-like snake surged out of the swamp, hissing and swirling. It had a thick body and huge head. Daniel stopped and swung his sword, ready for action, but the snake only slithered back into the swamp, submerging itself in the dark, misty water.

'Did you see that?' said Daniel, apprehensively. 'I frightened it.'

Buddy Wizard smiled. 'Are you certain of that, Master Daniel?'

'Not really,' replied Daniel, moving closer to Buddy.

They arrived at an arched doorway surrounded by ivy. Daylight was fading fast. Buddy Wizard looked up to the sky. 'We must enter now – and quickly,' he said.

They passed through the archway, stepping onto a winding staircase and into darkness. Suddenly, the sword shone and glowed, turning magically into a shining sceptre. Daniel held it up high, lighting up the walls on each side of the narrow staircase. Step by step they crept up, higher and higher, until they reached a narrow, faintly lit hallway. In front of them was a doorway masked in cobwebs. A small gust of wind rustled the cobwebs and a large black spider crawled across the silky strands.

Daniel jumped backwards.

'Yuk, there's a spider as big as my hand.'

Buddy Wizard blew at the spider's web, parting it. The hairy creature swayed back and forth, clinging on to its web until it was forced to scuttle back onto the wall and retreat gracefully into a hole.

'I hope it stays there,' said Daniel, hurrying past. The doorway led into a wide passage. Ahead, Daniel saw shadowy wooden cages. He lowered his sceptre and it turned back into a sword.

'That's magic,' Daniel said. 'Look, it's now a sword again.'

'Shush, Daniel, said Buddy. 'Listen.'

'I can hear voices,' said Daniel. 'Are they the kids from my school?'

He stopped in the candlelit area that housed the rows of cages. He could hear screams. Rats scampered along the gangway, weaving in and out of the stone crevices, boldly venturing near the cages. The girls from Middleton High screamed as they tried in vain to ward off the menacing rodents. Boys whimpered, grabbing hold of the bars in the cages, struggling to force open the strong gates.

Suddenly, a ghost appeared from nowhere, calling out, 'Nasty bullies!' It flashed past the cages, heading towards Daniel and Buddy. The ghost stopped, squinting into the darkness. Seconds later it darted back and raced along the gangway, laughing. 'Bullies,' the ghost sang. 'We must capture more.'

Buddy Wizard slipped hastily through the doorway. 'Quick,' he said. 'We must go.' They approached the cages.

'Look, there's Daniel Brady,' said one girl, looking amazed. The caged children rushed to look. Small beams of light flew from Buddy Wizard's hands. The light struck the cage doors, springing the doors open. One by one the boys and girls scuttled out of the cages into the gangway.

Buddy Wizard and Daniel led the children from the

dungeons, through the dark doorway, along the passage to the stairway, down the steps. They emerged onto the path at the side of the swamp. The light had faded. Daniel held up his shining sceptre and showed them the way ahead. Each child scurried past Daniel to join Buddy Wizard along the side of the swamp. The water rippled and glistened under a thousand stars, and a full moon shone. The sound of splashing filled the air as the swamp hissed and bubbled.

'Come quickly,' Buddy Wizard called out.

Daniel held the sceptre high, constantly looking behind him. 'Hurry, and keep together,' he told them.

They entered the tunnel leading up to the manor. The sound of thunder rumbled through the walls of the narrow tunnel as the children scampered along the stone passageway. Higher and higher they ran, their footsteps echoing. They sped out into the candlelit passage then stopped, staring at Buddy Wizard and looking around at the maze of passageways that confronted them. Daniel lowered his sceptre and once again held a shiny sword.

Daniel saw three ghostly figures coming after them. 'Go quickly, Buddy. We're being followed!'

They ran along the passageway, changing direction until Buddy Wizard stopped, pointing to two statues of soldiers on either side of an arch. One figure held a shining cross and the other held a dagger.

'Go that way,' said Buddy Wizard urgently. 'The Punishers are near. Don't forget that you are known as bullies.'

'Be on your guard,' warned Daniel. 'They may come for you again.'

227

The Punishers flew along the corridor as the children ran between the statues, through an arch and disappeared. Buddy Wizard began to fade as the last girl darted through the archway, spurred on by Daniel, who waited behind her.

'*Not you,*' screamed a voice. Daniel felt a force pulling him back.

'Let me go!' Daniel called out. He was about to face the wrath of the Punishers.

The rescued boys and girls burst out of the school courtyard, frantically running for safety. The school seemed deserted. They eventually ran into the main hall – and came face to face with five hundred school pupils having assembly.

The teachers all stood up. Mr Shaw and Miss White jumped off the stage and ran towards the frightened group.

'Hurry – this way,' Mr Shaw called, beckoning the pupils to go with him.

A hum of excited voices erupted in the hall as Mr North ran out with Mr Shaw to call the police, closing the doors behind them.

Miss Griffin sobbed. 'They're back safely – thank God.'

Teachers looked worriedly out of the windows, as though they expected visitors. The suspense heightened when sirens sounded in the distance. The sirens grew louder and louder until police cars and ambulances raced through the school gates and into the school car park. Police officers rushed into the reception area. At the same time, shocked pupils began to walk out of the hall. Some sniggered nervously, while others were pale and scared, but one pupil wanted desperately to get closer to what was happening and learn more.

Billy Riley edged his way past other pupils, stealthily moving nearer the staffroom.

'Hold it lad,' ordered a policeman, pointing to the other pupils. 'You're supposed to be going the other way.'

Riley told the truth. 'Sorry, but I need to speak to Mr Shaw.'

The police officer shooed Billy away. 'Not at the moment, lad.'

'Who wants to see me?' asked Mr Shaw, standing at the staffroom door.

'I do, sir.'

'What do you want, Billy?'

'I wanted to tell you about some strange things that have happened to me, sir – and Daniel Brady.'

'Such as?' asked Mr Shaw.

Riley hastily told him.

'I didn't know you were involved,' said Mr Shaw. 'The children have just told us about their ordeal – about the ghosts and dungeons. Daniel rescued the boys and girls, but hasn't returned with them.'

Billy didn't answer; he just ran after the rescued children being taken to the waiting ambulances. He hurried along the line of children, asking them what had happened. He fired question after question at them before they all filed out of the building.

'Billy Riley, get back here!' shouted Mr Shaw. But Billy Riley kept going, hiding among the pupils.

# Chapter 25

Billy Riley rushed to the crossover link – where he thought Daniel should be. He stopped hesitantly near the doorway, gazing across the lawn into the bushes that concealed the small statue on the wall and the clasped hands holding a cross. His mind went back to the frightening lessons he had learned – the scary moments of the coal mine, the chimney, the dormitory, and the ghost taking him to the graves. Billy walked cautiously out across the grass, towards the statue, knowing he had to be brave. Without thinking any more about it, he pushed hard on the statue. In a flash of light, he disappeared.

Billy opened his eyes and stared up at an old building with a towering roof that seemed to touch the black clouds that hung from the night sky. The air was humid and warm. Billy hesitated, unsure where to go and what to do. He spotted movement near the trees. He looked twice and instinctively shot away from the creepy shadow. Glancing back, he caught a glimpse of something heading his way. He began walking faster and faster, before sprinting up to the old building.

Billy hid in a doorway, puffing and panting. 'I–I don't believe this. Maybe I shouldn't have tried to come here. Something's chasing me.'

He leaned against a door and it gave way, sending him reeling into a dark room. A plaque hanging on the wall shone. Its words glared out at him.

'Oh no,' he blubbered. 'It's a plaque – the same one as in our school.' He peered closer, focusing on the reassuring words. *If there is darkness, I will provide you with comfort and light.*

'Please, God, I will be good,' pleaded Billy, rubbing his eyes, trying to see across the room. He headed towards the light, then cautiously looked through a doorway into a candlelit passageway. Billy had a feeling he had been here before. He edged along the passageway, his back to the wall, trying to make himself as small as possible. He crept from doorway to doorway, fleeting visions of ghosts crossing his mind. He could see flashes of light in the distance and hear the occasional scream.

I can hear water, thought Billy. His eyes gradually adjusted, and he saw a glittering stream flowing fast near the path. Another sound distracted him, and he glanced behind. In the distance he could see ghostly figures coming his way. Billy hid in the shadows. He stood frozen to the spot, his heart racing. Who's out there? he wondered. Someone was lurking nearby. Out of the darkness, a ghost loomed.

'Arghh, get away!' Billy staggered back. 'Leave me alone.'

But that was the last word he spoke – he fell into the fast-flowing water and was swept away.

The water gushed along, carrying Billy into a dark tunnel. He held his head high above the swirling water, which bounced him around through dips and troughs. Eventually, he was spewed out into a moonlit lake. Billy clambered out of the water, coughing and spluttering. It was dusk. Flashes of lightning lit up a path leading to a stream. He struggled to his feet, his clothes heavy, with water dripping onto the sodden grass.

Billy faltered and staggered feverishly along the side of a stream that led to a high wall next to a swamp. He heard the water rippling close to his feet, and his body trembled. The reflection from the stream lit up the narrow pathway next to a wall. Suddenly, a huge wave splashed over him. He stumbled into the wall and something gave way. He fell through a door, landing face down in a huge vat of an odd white powdery substance.

'Help!' spluttered Billy, struggling in the dark.

He could feel his body sinking. He twisted and turned frantically, until he realised he could stand upright. He laughed nervously, looking at the white substance that stuck to his clothes and covered his body.

'Keep calm,' he muttered. 'Please God – get me out of this, I'll be good.'

He staggered out of the white powder and grabbed a rail, but to his horror it snapped and he plunged back in and was now completely covered. Once again, he struggled to his feet, clambered out of the vat like trough, and headed to the doorway.

The water bubbled furiously as Billy stepped outside. It was dark. He wiped the wet powder from his eyes. The moon burst through the black clouds and lit up the narrow pathway. A fountain of water surged high in the night sky and dropped on to the glimmering swamp. Frightened, Billy sprinted along the side of the steep walls, eager to escape the wrath of the bubbling water. He turned into the archway that led up to a stairway then ran. He didn't know where he was running, or what he was running from; he just ran, his footsteps echoing. He reached the top and continued into a room filled with cages.

Daniel sat behind the sturdy wooden bars in his cage, wondering who on earth was making such a noise. Billy Riley emerged, still covered in white, from the cobwebbed doorway and into the dungeons, puffing and panting. Daniel was now confronted with a ghastly white image stooping nearby.

Billy Riley lurched towards Daniel, trying to catch his breath. Daniel held up his chain and pendant, pointing it towards the white crusty image of Billy.

'Keep back, you fiend,' he said shakily. But nothing happened. The menacing white figure of Billy came closer.

'It's me, Billy Riley.'

Daniel reared back. 'What did you say?'

Billy spluttered behind the white coating. 'It's me, Billy Riley. I've … come … to … rescue … you.'

The white coating hung heavy on his wet clothes. Billy stumbled a few paces then slumped against the wooden poles of the cages.

Daniel laughed. 'You've come to rescue me?'

Billy's stiff hands grappled with the heavy timber. He tried to manoeuvre the bar.

'Someone's coming, Billy,' said Daniel. 'Hurry up.'

A strange screeching noise began to echo through the

dungeons.

Billy's neck creaked. 'I'm … a bit … stiff.'

The screeching came closer.

'Sounds like trouble,' said Daniel. 'Quick, hide.'

Billy carried on trying to wriggle the bar free. In the meantime Daniel spotted a ghost. He began furiously waving his hand, trying to warn Billy. The ghost stood watching, tilting his head from side to side, seemingly confused about the white figure grappling with the bar. Daniel looked into Billy's eyes, signalling him to look behind. Billy finally acknowledged Daniel and turned to look. He stared in horror at the ghost, and panicked, groaning and grunting. The ghost was surprised and drifted back a couple of metres. Billy shook with fright, but instinctively held his white arms out and staggered towards the ghost.

'That's it,' said Daniel. 'Billy Frankenstein.'

The ghost drifted further back then vanished.

'You did it, Billy.' Bits of white began falling from Billy's body and face. Daniel pushed his face against the bars. 'Come on, get me out.'

Billy began to pull the heavy wooden bar again. But without warning, two more mean-looking ghosts appeared. Daniel moved cautiously back.

'Billy, look out,' Daniel warned him. It was too late. A fierce gust of wind lifted him up, pinning him to the wooden rafters. Daniel looked on helplessly as Billy struggled, his clothes patchy white and still wet.

'Let me go,' Billy cried. 'I promise not to be a bully.'

'Oh! You want to come down?' bellowed a ghost.

Billy suddenly dropped upside down from the rafters and hung by one foot.

'And along came a spider,' cackled another ghost. A monster spider crawled out of a dark corner, making its way along the rafter.

Daniel wrenched at the bars in horror. 'Leave him alone, you big, slimy, ugly thing!'

One ghost simply turned to Daniel and snarled.

'Let us all vote for Riley's future,' came a voice from several metres away. It was Buddy Wizard, standing with his hands on his hips. The ghosts answered swiftly and together they blew Buddy Wizard off his feet. The ghosts then burst into laughter and so a battle began along the passageway.

Billy dangled precariously beneath the huge spider. Daniel gripped his chain and prayed, but nothing happened. In desperation, Daniel removed his chain and called out to Billy, 'Catch!'

The chain spun through the air and Billy grabbed it.

'Hold on to it tightly,' suggested Daniel. 'It may protect you too.'

Billy held the chain tightly and closed his eyes.

The spider shuffled along the beam. It stayed motionless, ready to pounce. Sweat trickled down Billy's neck. He clutched tighter at the chain. The spider pounced, spinning its web furiously around Billy.

'Help me!' pleaded Billy, struggling to break free.

Daniel wrestled with the cage door, trying to reach for his sword, which lay on the ground. It was no good. He remained powerless.

Billy lifted his arm, gripped the chain and started punching the spider. The chain swished back and forth in his hand, hitting the spider. Suddenly a spark flickered and the spider's body lit up. A flame appeared. The spider leaped back onto the beam and scuttled into the dark corner of the roof, its backside smoking. Billy pulled his arms free from the web, unhitched his feet, then dropped to the floor.

The two ghosts saw Billy break free. They left Buddy Wizard and moved fast to Billy, lifting him up, tossing him towards Daniel's cage. The bar slid back. Billy went in and the cage door slammed shut. The ghosts zoomed off with Buddy Wizard.

Billy groaned. 'Get these cobwebs and white muck off me – please Daniel.'

They tugged at the white strands and heaved at the twine, not noticing the people gathering outside their cage. One by one, tiny ghosts of boys and girls dressed in rags appeared and began to giggle at Daniel and Billy, grappling with cobwebs and the white paste.

Then Billy spotted them. His eyes nearly popped out of his head as one girl spoke.

'Are you both bullies?' she asked.

Daniel, on the other hand, was interested in something else. 'Where's my chain?' he asked anxiously.

'I dropped it out there,' replied Billy, bowing his head. They looked at the pendant and chain lying next to the sword. 'I'm sorry.'

'We don't like bullies,' scowled a girl. 'Some of my

friends want to punish you.'

'We're not bullies,' Daniel said humbly.

*'He is!'* screamed a boy ghost, pointing at Billy.

'No,' replied Daniel, 'not any more. He's healed.'

'Once a bully, always a bully,' shrieked the girl. They stared, angrily nodding in agreement, then a taller ghost appeared. The cage bar slid off, the door swung open, and Billy was sucked out of the cage. Daniel was propelled backwards and the door closed.

The ghosts all surrounded Billy then disappeared with him. Daniel stood helplessly, listening to the echoes of the children's laughter.

It was silent except for the trickle of water along the passageway and the scuffling of rats. Daniel sat on the cold ground, trying to think of a way to escape, but it was hopeless.

A few lonely hours went by. Daniel sat dozing, listening to distant cries and moans. The strange noises were a constant reminder that he was not alone in this unearthly dungeon. Finally, the welcome figure of Buddy Wizard appeared outside the cage. He picked up the chain and sword. The bar on the door slid sideways and Daniel rushed out.

'Sorry to disappoint you,' said a boy's voice. 'I am not your buddy.'

His face began to change. 'The Punishers sent me.'

A white eagle flew above Daniel. The massive bird swooped and lifted Daniel up in its great claws. It carried him off along the passageway, the boy ghost trailing behind.

They flew up the stairway, in and out of passageways and on to the great hall where dozens of ghosts had gathered. Everyone watched as the bird entered carrying Daniel, dangling helplessly in its claws. He was carried to the far end of the hall and dropped at the feet of two Punishers, who guarded a cage.

Daniel noticed a face pressed against the bars of the cage.

'Billy,' he asked, 'is that you?'

'Yes,' whispered Billy, shaking. 'I'm terrified. Get me out of 'ere – please.'

'Silence!' yelled a Punisher.

'Bring forth the accused,' came another voice.

The ghosts parted, revealing the three ghost judges at the end of the hall. The mean-looking male judge sat in the centre, between the two female judges. Billy Riley edged back out of sight.

Daniel stood, boldly facing the judges. 'Why am I a prisoner?' he asked.

'Silence! Bring forth the accused.'

The bar slid from the cage and the door opened. Billy Riley was sucked forward next to Daniel, facing the judges.

'Tell us your name,' roared the male judge, pointing to Billy.

'Riley – B-B-Billy Riley. Please let me go. I promise not to bully.'

The male ghost snarled. 'For hundreds of years we have tracked your kind – the sneaky kind, perpetrators of ridicule, the silent bully, the coward. We have tried in vain to catch bullies like you to educate them, but without great success, until now. And, thanks to Daniel Brady, we will succeed.'

'Buddy Wizard wouldn't lie,' interrupted Daniel. 'I'm not the descendant of a wicked man.'

'No, you are not,' acknowledged the ghost. He thrust his finger towards Billy and all eyes followed. 'Riley is the descendant!'

Daniel gasped. 'You, Billy, it's you – you're part of the prophecy.'

Billy went white. 'What?'

'Take a look at your ancestor,' boomed the ghost. The room began to fill with men, women and children dressed in rags. They waited below a raised wooden platform, looking up at three men and three women standing on the platform with ropes placed around their necks. A buzz of chatter filled the air. The ghost spoke again.

'Look closely, Billy Riley – your ancestor ordered the execution of these poor souls he falsely called criminals.'

The six were whisked into the air. A minute later they hung, lifeless.

'Look again, Billy Riley,' said the ghost. A graveyard appeared before Billy's eyes, full of small crosses. 'These poor children were innocent, yet they were bullied and cruelly treated by your wicked ancestor.'

The light faded and the male ghost judge leaned over, looking down at Billy. 'Many died this way, yet only a few rose from their graves. We could not catch your ancestor, Riley, but we trapped others and punished them – a death for a death. Some of us roamed the castle and manor. But they were demolished. Now we can do our work again in

Middleton High.'

'That is true,' Buddy Wizard's mother said. 'But there will be changes.'

She looked all around then snapped, 'We cannot all enter Middleton High.'

Daniel and Billy felt the floor tremble beneath their feet.

'Well spoken, Mother,' said Buddy Wizard. 'But first we must free Daniel and Billy – they mean us no harm.'

'*No!*' roared the angry male judge. 'We must vote.'

'So shall it be,' was the reply.

'But, before you vote,' appealed Buddy Wizard, 'forget the past, look to the future. Look at the reformed Billy Riley and his friend, Daniel. I have witnessed the change in Billy Riley.'

Daniel and Billy were whisked into the cage and the door slammed shut. The ghosts stirred, preparing to vote. However, Buddy Wizard had a different idea. Discreetly, he wandered to the rear of the cage.

'Daniel, Billy,' whispered Buddy, 'step out of the cage, quietly.'

Daniel and Billy began their escape. The sturdy poles were bending, making an opening big enough for them to squeeze through.

'This way,' said Buddy.

They crept out of the great hall. Buddy insisted they make haste. 'Run back through the dungeons, out to the swamps and through the tunnel – and take these.'

He handed Daniel the sword with the shiny chain and pendant. 'I will meet you there soon.'

# Chapter 26

Daniel and Billy raced along the winding passageways through the dungeons to the top of the stairway where Daniel raised his sword. It became a shining sceptre to light their path. They ran down the winding steps, through the archway and out into the sunlit swamp.

'Be careful here,' warned Daniel. He led the way along the narrow path.

'There's something in the water,' whispered Billy. They looked fearfully at the calm water, disturbed only by the odd ripple and glistening in the sunlight.

'Shush,' Daniel said. 'I can hear something.'

Suddenly, the water bubbled and swished. The dragon snake stirred. Its huge body swirled out of the water. It surged upwards, rising high above Daniel and Billy. The boys stood still, staring up at the huge reptile.

Daniel raised his gleaming sword in defence, thrusting it towards the dragon snake. The reptile drew its head back, ready to strike, when they heard another noise nearby.

'It's the Punishers!' Billy shouted.

'But they're not supposed to come here!' said Daniel, still holding the sword.

The dragon snake turned, glaring at the pursuing

Punishers. It fell back into the water and swam towards them. It reared up out of the water then splashed back in, sending water cascading onto to the Punishers and washing them into the swamp.

'Quick! Let's get out of here!' yelled Daniel. They raced along the narrow pathway until Daniel stopped. 'We've gone past the tunnel.'

They searched the undergrowth for the entrance – then something grabbed Billy's trouser leg. He leaped back. Daniel held his sword at the ready. He shuddered at the cluster of giant crabs surrounding Billy.

Daniel swung his sword, ferociously striking each crab with a broad swipe. He smashed a crab onto the wall and knocked another into the water.

'Run, Billy!' insisted Daniel. 'Go to the tunnel entrance.'

Billy didn't hesitate. He ran through the archway with Daniel close behind. 'That really scared me,' gasped Billy stopping for breath. 'I don't like snakes or crabs.' The glare from the sceptre lit up the murky walls.

'Wow, that's magic,' remarked Billy.

'Shush,' interrupted Daniel. 'Keep still – I can see ghosts.'

The light from the sceptre began to fade, and white smoke began to drift towards them. They didn't move, trying to wave the smoke away.

'What's happening?' asked Billy.

They stared at a line of ghostly-looking soldiers walking towards them, carrying flaming torches. Billy darted behind Daniel. 'Those creepy things are coming towards us! We're trapped.'

'We're not trapped,' Daniel said, grabbing Billy's hand. 'Hold on.'

The soldiers came closer and closer. The sound of heavy footsteps thundered through the tunnel. Daniel walked boldly towards the soldiers, tugging Billy with him. The soldiers kept coming. Daniel held his breath as they marched straight through him, showing no fear or direction on their rugged faces and cold eyes. They passed quickly, marching off into the distance.

'You can open your eyes now,' suggested Daniel. Billy heard a snap: a crab claw had narrowly missed his leg. The startled Billy dashed past Daniel and kept on running. He raced out of the tunnel and into the old manor.

Daniel called to him. 'Stop, Billy! It's okay now.'

But Billy kept on running. He ran along the candlelit passageway – straight into the path of two Punishers. They picked him up and carried him in the air between them. Daniel ran after them, but ran straight into more Punishers. They swooped down, grabbed Daniel and carried him off too, along the passageway behind Billy.

The Punishers hauled Daniel and Billy back into the great hall, leaving them on the ground in front of a small audience of ghosts.

'Billy Riley,' growled a loud voice. 'You have been found guilty.'

All eyes turned to the three judges. The nasty old male judge stretched forward and scowled. 'You have been found guilty of bullying, along with others at your school. We have not forgotten the sins of your past relative.'

'But that's not Billy's fault,' pleaded Daniel.

The old ghost glared. 'Ah, young Brady,' he scoffed. 'The interfering menace.'

Daniel replied defiantly, 'Wait until Buddy Wizard comes to save me.'

The old ghost chuckled. 'He is already here to witness your fate. He cannot help you now.'

Daniel looked for Buddy Wizard and finally spotted him.

The old ghost turned his attention to Billy. 'Your punishment will be a test, Billy Riley, to prove you have changed your ways. You will be tested along with many other children. You will be observed when you least expect it.'

The old ghost turned to Daniel. 'Since we have not entered your time for two hundred years, we cannot judge what is happening there. The one you call Buddy Wizard is your ancestor William Brady.'

'Yes, Daniel,' agreed Buddy, appearing next to Daniel's side. 'I am Will Brady – Buddy Wizard, to you. From the time you touched the tree I knew you were part of me, and part of the future – a future that appears to be changing.'

The old ghost spoke again. 'Master Will has suggested that nasty children turn into nasty adults, and he claims that this is a problem, so we have agreed to search for nasty children and educate them.'

'Rather them than me,' interrupted Billy.

The old ghost forced a smile. 'Master Will – or, should I say, Master Buddy Wizard – return them home before I change my mind.'

There was a hum of agreement and disapproval as the ghosts watched Buddy Wizard throw a twinkling of stars around Daniel and Billy. All three vanished from the great hall.

'You must go,' Buddy Wizard insisted. 'Things are not finished here. There are always angry Punishers craving revenge. Guard your pendant and chain well, Daniel.'

'I will,' Daniel agreed, gripping the chain tightly.

Buddy turned to Billy. 'And you, Master Riley, have learned a valuable lesson. But you need a solid reminder for the future.'

Billy felt something slither over his shoulder then wrap itself around his neck.

'No, not a chain,' he said in horror. 'No, please, not a chain!'

He looked at Daniel's chain and then breathed a sigh of relief. 'It's not the same chain but I've got a pendant the same as yours.'

'Quickly,' Buddy Wizard said, 'you must go.' But as he spoke there was a thump, and the floor shook. Suddenly footprints materialised in the dust, and a monster appeared. The monster ghost laughed, then bellowed out some familiar hideous words: 'Tell all the bullies to change, or beware – or they will face me to give them a scare.'

Daniel flinched. 'He's real. Help!'

Daniel signalled Billy. Together they ran to the archway and vanished.

They reappeared in the garden by the crossover link at Middleton High.

Daniel smiled. 'It's snowed! And it's daylight.'

'We'd better creep inside,' Billy said nervously.

They crunched carefully through the snow, looking back.

'Oh no,' Daniel gulped. 'The teachers will see this. Look at our footprints.' They reached the door and Daniel pushed the door handle down. 'It's locked. And school seems really quiet. Where is everyone?'

'I've no idea.'

'I think the school is closed.'

Unexpectedly a loud whirring noise came from the sky. A helicopter zoomed overhead. It swooped down towards Daniel and Billy. The helicopter hovered above them, sending out a deafening thump, thump, thump from the circling propellers.

'You don't think it's looking for us, do you?' asked Billy, anxiously.

'It must be.'

The helicopter rose in the sky and veered off into the distance.

'Quick!' Daniel said. 'We've got to get out of this courtyard.'

They jumped up onto the dustbins. Billy knelt down and Daniel stood on him to reach up. Daniel clutched the top of the roof then hauled himself up to the fascia and onto the flat roof. He then stretched down to help Billy. They ran across the flat roof then dropped down to the ground. They dashed towards the school entrance, climbed over the gate, then dropped, relieved, onto the snowy pavement, eager to make their way home.

'Come back to my house,' suggested Daniel.

'Can I?'

'Yeah, sure.'

'Okay.'

They hadn't gone very far when they saw a group of boys and girls.

'Hey, you two,' shouted a boy. 'The police are looking for you.'

Daniel and Billy didn't take much notice. They already knew the police wanted to question them. They carried on walking, past another group of boys and girls who also called out.

'There's a big reward out for you two,' one girl declared.

'It's really them,' said another girl. Daniel and Billy strode past, ignoring them.

'Look, they're back.'

'It really is them.'

Daniel and Billy kept on walking.

Gradually the light began to fade and snowflakes began to fall as they trudged through the snow, heading towards Old Furrow Way. One by one the streetlights came alive, illuminating the millions of white flakes dropping from the heavy sky. They walked past children holding lanterns and singing carols. They saw colourfully lit Christmas trees and decorations, reminding them that Christmas wasn't far away.

'Daniel,' called a boy running past. 'Are you okay?'

'Yeah, thanks.' *Why is he asking me if I'm okay?*

'You live near here, don't you?' Billy asked, flicking

the snow from his hair.

'Yeah,' Daniel replied unenthusiastically. Soon another boy approached them.

'Hi, Daniel! I'm so pleased to see you.'

'What's going on, Tyler? And where's Sophie?'

'Don't you know?' replied Tyler. 'You've been missing for days. You're a hero, man. You freed the kids. They've been telling the police how they were kidnapped and held in a dungeon. Look behind you.'

Daniel and Billy looked. Lots of their fellow students waved back at them. Tyler threw his hands in the air. 'You saved the other kids. The police can't work it out. A crazy professor turned up with a couple of fanatical ghost-finders to look for you. We told them all about what happened and they believed us.'

'They got to Sophie,' said Tyler.

'Who's got to Sophie?'

'The ghosts—'

Billy interrupted. 'We can't go back!'

Tyler raised his hands. 'Who said anything about going back?'

Daniel stopped in his tracks. 'We're not going to leave her there.'

'Let me finish; I meant the ghosts have got to Sophie. She can't stop talking about ghosts. She's been bragging about your dreams and the ghosts she saw with you. Now all the kids think she's really cool. The teachers and everyone keep questioning her.'

Daniel picked up a snowball.

Tyler ran.

'You idiot,' Daniel said, throwing the snowball at him. Sirens sounded in the distance.

'Let's leg it,' Billy suggested. Daniel nodded and they ran into Old Furrow Way followed by a group of kids. Two police cars with flashing lights also arrived, trying to edge their way through.

Daniel beckoned Billy. 'It's just ahead. Come on!'

He ran into the driveway, Billy close behind. The children stopped and milled around in the street. 'Wait, we only want to know what happened.'

The police cars came to a halt and officers began to force their way through the crowd.

'Listen,' Billy said. 'What's that noise?'

Another helicopter flew overhead. It fluttered and circled, shining a beam down onto the ground. The children's faces lit up among the falling snow and the police officers moved in, hustling them away from Daniel's driveway. Within minutes the crowd had dispersed. The helicopter circled once more before flying off.

It was quiet – except for the sound of carol singers.

'There are people at my front door,' commented Daniel.

'I didn't realise we've been gone for days. It didn't seem that long,' Billy said.

'I know,' replied Daniel. 'They'll be worried. Oh well, let's face the wrinklies.'

They approached the house, which was in darkness except for a porch light shining on a small Christmas tree. The carol singers stopped singing. One of them spun around.

'Merry Christmas, Daniel. Merry Christmas, William,' said a man. Daniel knew his voice. He was partially obscured by the light from the lantern.

'Who's there?' asked Daniel. The group turned around, holding up their lanterns, revealing their faces. Mr Shaw and Miss White, Miss Griffin, Miss Tubble, Mr North – and Sophie and Tyler.

Sophie didn't hesitate. She rushed at Daniel and gave him a big hug. 'I knew you would make it,' she whispered.

'Oh my God, it is you two!' Miss White exclaimed. She blinked then wiped her eyes. 'You're back! We have been frantic about you.'

Mr Shaw stepped forward. 'You're obviously brave lads. The police will want to interview you two, but it's Christmas Eve, so they'll just have to wait.'

'What?' Daniel shrieked. 'Christmas Eve?'

Suddenly, the front door opened.

'I'm sorry,' Mrs Brady sighed. 'I'm not in the Christmas spirit – but here's a donation anyway.'

She placed some money in the box without looking at anyone, then asked, 'What on earth was going on with those helicopters?'

Before anyone could answer, Chip came running through the hall and leaped into the air. He landed in Daniel's arms.

'Chip! Chip!' Daniel said, delighted, cuddling him. 'How are you, boy?'

Mrs Brady stared in disbelief.

'Daniel, Daniel, it's you!' she cried. 'It's really you! Thank God!'

She ran outside and hugged him then rushed back into the house, shouting, 'Dad, Emily, quick! Daniel's back – he's home!'

Daniel cuddled Chip. The group of teachers, along with Sophie and Tyler, walked away, leaving Billy standing alone. Chip began to growl. Daniel whispered in his ear. The little dog wagged his tail then lifted his paw for Billy to shake.

'That's it,' Daniel joked. 'You're friends for life now.'

Mr Brady stood in the doorway. 'Never mind that! Daniel, what the hell happened to you? Where have you been? We heard you two went back in time. How did you do that? The police mentioned something about ghosts. We couldn't get to the bottom of anything. We've been worried to death. Your mum hasn't slept. Not eating. Couldn't you have contacted us? Everyone's been looking for you. We've heard strange things about you and the school. You then turn up as if nothing has happened. You've got some explaining to do. Is this the boy, William, we've heard about?'

Daniel nodded humbly.

'Come on in, both of you. We'll contact his parents.'

Emily waited at the door. 'Daniel – it is you, thank God. You really scared us. Where have you been?'

Daniel's dad ushered them in and closed the door. 'The police will be coming soon to speak to you both about where you have been and who else is involved.'

The rest of the evening was a bit hectic in Daniel's house, but elsewhere remained peaceful and quiet in Old Furrow Way.

*** 

Father Christmas was coming. For most children, tonight was the best night of the year. The night was full of excitement. Bedtime came and went. Jack Frost struck everywhere, leaving his frosty footprints, and only left when Christmas Day arrived.

'Look, Chip,' Daniel said, yawning. 'There's a robin in the garden. We'd better give it some food or else it might die.'

The little dog looked out of the bedroom window and whined.

***

Somewhere on the west side of the city, a young girl was also feeding a robin. The tiny bird hopped across the snowy ground towards the girl. Bravely, it came very close, but she began to sob and didn't take much notice of it. The robin chirped. The girl wiped her blurry eyes. She focused on the bird, which was tossing something up in the air with its beak. The object landed in the snow and the girl bent down to pick it up. The robin flew off, skimming low to the ground. She picked up the shiny object and studied it closely. I wonder what she saw?

*THE END*